Border Line

Robert J. Conley

Thorndike Press • Chivers Press
Waterville, Maine USA Bath, England

This Large Print edition is published by Thorndike Press, USA and by Chivers Press, England.

Published in 2003 in the U.S. by arrangement with Cherry Weiner Literary Agency.

Published in 2003 in the U.K. by arrangement with the author.

U.S. Hardcover 0-7862-4299-X (Western Series)
U.K. Hardcover 0-7540-8962-2 (Chivers Large Print)
U.K. Softcover 0-7540-8963-0 (Camden Large Print)

The text of this Large Print edition is unabridged.
Other aspects of the book may vary from the original edition.

Set in 16 pt. Plantin by Myrna S. Raven.

Printed in the United States on permanent paper.

British Library Cataloguing-in-Publication Data available

Library of Congress Cataloging-in-Publication Data

Conley, Robert J.
    Border line / Robert J. Conley.
       p. cm.
    ISBN 0-7862-4299-X (lg. print : hc : alk. paper)
    1. Cherokee Indians — Fiction.   2. Racially mixed people
— Fiction.   3. Gold — Transportation — Fiction.
4. Oklahoma — Fiction.   5. Outlaws — Fiction.   6. Large
type books.   I. Title.
PS3553.O494 B67 2003
    813'.54—dc21
                                                    2002068704

For Earl Squyres

Prologue

Katharine Lacey tossed a bale of hay down in the corral for her old milk cow and broke it open. Then she stood back and wiped the sweat from her forehead with the back of her arm. The work on her Iowa farm was just too much for her alone. Then she heard the sound of an approaching horse. She turned to look down toward the road, and she saw Josh Towers riding in her direction. She walked out to meet him, a puzzled look on her face.

"Good morning, Mr. Towers," she said. "What brings you all the way out here?"

Towers pulled his horse to a halt and dismounted.

"Miss Lacey," he said, "I've got a letter here for you."

"A letter?"

"Yeah, well, I know it's unusual. I mean for me to ride out like this to deliver a letter. I don't ordinarily do it, and I wouldn't have done it this time, except I'm really embarrassed about this. I mean, it shouldn't happen with the U.S. mail."

He reached into his inside coat pocket

and pulled out a letter.

"What do you mean?" said Katharine.

"We were cleaning up the office this morning," said Towers. "We moved the desk out, and, well, we found this on the floor back there. I guess it had fallen down behind the desk. Been there for a little over three years, it looks like. I'm really sorry about that."

He handed the letter to Katharine, and he remounted his horse and started to turn around to head back for town.

"I'm really sorry, Miss Lacey," he said, and he rode away.

Katharine looked at the envelope.

"Ben," she said out loud, and she tore open the envelope and unfolded the letter to read.

Dear Mom and Dad and Sis,

I just want to let you know where Im at and that all is well with me. This is abaot the first chanse Ive had to rite and I guess it will be a short one you now how I am at riting. Well im down hear in Texas of all places and Im a partner in a real horse ranch. We call it the LWM for Lacey Walker and McClellan. Those are my pards Dhu Walker thats the Walker and he is a

Cherake Indian. There not wild like you mite think. We met in the war. And the M is for Herd McClellan and I have a wife now his daughter Mary Beth. We have just had a little baby a girl and her name is Nellie Bell. I sure do miss all of you and wish I could get back home to see you or you could get down this way either one. Rite to me and tell me how you are all of you or as these Texans say you all.

Your son and brother,
Benjamin Franklin Lacey

ps you can rite to me at the LWM Ranch in Preston Texas. were not really in Preston but we get are mail there.

Chapter 1

Preston, Texas, wasn't much, but it was the closest excuse for a town to the LWM Ranch. It was the place mail got delivered to and sent out from. It had the nearest general store, and it had a saloon. It didn't have a church yet, but there was an arbor where church meetings were sometimes held. There was talk of building a school, but that had been going on for some years. Preston had escaped most of the violence of the type that had taken place in Gainesville not too far away during the late war. Even so, there was still hostility there, hostility on the part of former rebels and rebel sympathizers toward people like Ben Lacey, Dhu Walker, the McClellans, and other Red River farmers and ranchers who had remained loyal to the Union during the war.

There was no law in Preston. The county sheriff's office was located in Gainesville. Occasionally there were patrols of Union cavalry. When any trouble occurred, someone either sent for the cavalry or sent for the sheriff from Gainesville to come and take care of the problem.

More likely, the people of Preston just took care of it themselves.

Ben Lacey wondered every time he went into Preston why in the world anyone had decided to build anything in that particular location. Every time he went to Preston, he decided that he would ask Herd McClellan the first chance he got why Preston was there, but he always forgot to ask.

Ben was riding into Preston with a purpose. He wanted to see if the mail delivery had arrived yet. Three years earlier he had written a letter to his parents and his sister back in Iowa, and he had not yet received a response. He was worried about them. He hadn't seen them since the beginning of the war, since the time he had joined the Union army and marched off to fight to hold the Union together. That had been four years ago, four long years. A great deal had happened since, Ben thought as he rode on. In his first major conflict, he had been taken prisoner by the Confederates, and he had been held along with a half-breed Cherokee named Dhu Walker.

Walker had been a member of the so-called Pin Indians, loyal to the Union, but when the Cherokee Chief John Ross had been forced to sign a treaty with the Confederacy, the Pin Indians had been told that they had become Confederates, and they had been marched into battle at Pea Ridge, Arkansas, to fight the Union forces. Some of the Pin Indians had refused to fight; some, in spite of what their commanders had told them, had fought against the Confederates.

Dhu Walker had been captured during the battle by Confederate forces and had been accused of being a turncoat. Ben hadn't liked the Indian at first. He had never known an Indian before, had never even seen one, and he didn't like the idea of the man having turned against his own side in the heat of battle. He hadn't fully understood the dilemma of the Pin Indians.

But when Dhu Walker had decided to escape, Ben had seen that his only chance was to stick with Dhu. They had escaped together, and Dhu had led Ben across the western border of Arkansas into the Cherokee Nation. Along the way Ben had told Dhu about the conversation in the officers' tent he had overheard while they had still been prisoners, about the orders Captain Gordon Early, known popularly as Old Harm, had received to go to Mexico to pick up a shipment of gold from some foreign country that was being sent to the

Confederacy, and to escort it back. The two had decided to go after Old Harm and the Confederate gold, and they had succeeded. They had succeeded so well that they had managed to hide the gold on the Red River farm of Herd McClellan, and no one had ever been the wiser.

Ben rode up expectantly to Elmer Tipton's general store on the main street of Preston and dismounted. He hitched his horse to the rail there and went inside, aware that some hostile eyes were watching him. Tipton was behind the counter in the store.

"Hello, Lacey," he said. "What can I do for you?"

"I've got a list here," said Ben. He dug the list out of his pocket and laid it on the counter. "But first, has the mail come in?"

"Yeah."

"Anything in there for me?"

"Letter here."

"Well, let me have it then," said Ben.

Tipton reached under the counter and found the letter. He laid it on the counter in front of Ben, and Ben took it anxiously. He wanted to tear it open and read. Instead he tucked it safely inside his shirt and waited while Tipton started going down the list and looking for the items to fill Ben's order. Ben tried hard to maintain a calm and casual demeanor, but he wasn't at all confident that he was being successful. He wanted to hurry Tipton along, yet he didn't want Tipton to know that he was anxious. Ben had learned that patience seemed to be thought of as the primary virtue in Texas, especially for a man.

"How's business at the big ranch?" asked Tipton.

"Oh, can't complain," said Ben. He wasn't about to tell Tipton anything specific. Tipton was one of those bitter former rebels. It was obvious that he resented the success of the LWM Ranch whose owners were all Yankees to his rebel mind. Actually, Ben thought, he, himself, was the only real Yankee of the three partners. He had enlisted on purpose in the Union army from his home in Iowa. Dhu Walker was a Cherokee, and the Cherokee Nation, at least the way Dhu told it, had tried to stay neutral. Once it had been dragged into what Dhu had called a white man's war, it had people fighting on both sides, sometimes shifting sides. And Herd McClellan had been a Red River farmer, originally from Missouri, who had just wanted to be left alone. However, to the defeated but stiff-necked rebels, they were a bunch of Yankees, and their success sure hadn't done their local reputations any good.

"Here you go," said Tipton, shoving a bundle of goods toward Ben. Ben paid the bill and picked up the package.

"Thanks," he said, and he walked out into the street. He tied the bundle behind his saddle and swung onto his horse's back, then rode out of town, again aware of hostile stares. Well out of town, well out of range of rebel eyes, he stopped the horse. He pulled the letter out of his shirt, tore it open, and started to read.

Dear Brother,

I'm sorry to be so slow answering your letter but I just received it. It was wonderful hearing from you. I just wish I had heard earlier, for Mama and Papa are both gone. Mama went first. She had been ill for some time. And Papa didn't last long after that. He didn't seem to care anymore, and it seemed like he just pined away. They died not knowing where you were, Bennie, not knowing if you were dead or alive. I don't blame you, and they didn't either. It was just the war and all.

Anyway it was sure good to hear from

you at last. I've been so busy. I've been trying to run this farm all by myself, but I can't seem to handle it on my own. Things are falling apart on me, I guess. Mr. Ord at the bank has agreed to buy the place and pay off the mortgage, but his offer is so low that there won't hardly be anything left over for me. I don't know what I'll do.

But that's enough of my problems. Everything will work out all right. It always does, doesn't it?

How about you? Married and a father! I can't hardly believe it. And part owner of a ranch in Texas, too. I'm so happy for you, and please give my love to your Mary Beth and to little Nellie Bell, my niece. One day I know I'll have the chance to meet them.

Please write again. It's so good to hear from you and to know that you're doing so well.

Love from your sister,
Katharine

Tears came to Ben's eyes as he read the letter. He tried to blink them back, but it was no use. He pulled the bandanna out of his hip pocket and wiped his eyes. He

16

took a couple of deep breaths and looked up into the sky.

"Oh, God," he said. "Oh, God."

He read through the letter again, and again he daubed at his eyes. Then he carefully refolded the letter, tucked it back inside his shirt, and started riding again toward the ranch.

In the time since the arrival of Ben and Dhu, Herd McClellan's Red River farm had undergone quite a transformation to become the LWM Ranch. The farm had become a horse ranch, and where there had been one house, there were three. Herd and Maude still lived in the same old house with Sam Ed, now a young man. It was amazing to Ben what four years had done to his young brother-in-law, what they had done to everyone. Ben, Mary Beth, and little Nellie Bell had their own small house just across the clearing from the old house, and up close to the gate — also new — was the log cabin in which Dhu Walker lived alone. The few horses they had used to start with had multiplied until they had become a fine herd. Far and wide it was known that the LWM had some of the finest horses available, and everyone thought that it was the army contracts that had brought such success to the LWM partners.

What they did not know about was the Confederate gold, the gold that Ben, Dhu, and the McClellans had intercepted and taken from Old Harm and his renegade Confederate soldiers. Over the years, Ben and Dhu had taken small amounts of the gold north and sold it for cash to a man that Dhu had known in the Cherokee Nation. A Cherokee mixed-blood named Nebo Drake, the man seemed to have an endless supply of ready cash. He bought the gold for less than its worth. Even so, it provided the partners with plenty of cash, and they didn't have to worry about explaining where they had gotten ahold of gold bars. After their first trip, Ben had asked Dhu about Drake.

"How does he get rid of the stuff?" he had said.

"Who knows?" said Dhu. "I guess he's got his ways."

Anyhow, the cash Drake paid for the gold had provided the LWM with ample working capital, and the general population around the area had simply assumed that the horse business had earned all the LWM money.

Ben didn't see anyone as he rode

through the main gate. He figured that the other men were all back at the corral working with the horses. The army liked their new stock to be already well trained, and the LWM had done its best to oblige. Ben went to his own house first, but he found no one at home, so he walked on over to the old house. As he approached the front door, Nellie Bell came running out to meet him.

"Daddy! Daddy!" she said.

Ben caught her up in his arms and held her close as her little arms circled his neck and squeezed him tight. He carried her back inside and found Mary Beth in the kitchen with Maude.

"Did you bring that stuff I asked you to?" said Maude.

"Oh, yeah," said Ben. "It's still out on my horse. I forgot. I'm sorry. I'll go get it."

"That's all right," said Maude. "You hold the baby. I'll fetch the stuff in."

Maude left, and Mary Beth stepped over to her husband and gave him a kiss on the cheek.

"I found Daddy," said Nellie Bell.

"You sure did," said Mary Beth. "That's good."

"I got a letter from Katharine," said Ben.

"Your sister?" said Mary Beth. "What's

wrong?" She could tell from the look on Ben's face and from the sound of his voice that the news had not been good.

"It's in my shirt," he said. "Read it."

He shifted Nellie Bell in his arms so that Mary Beth could get the letter. She took it to the table and sat down to read just as Maude came back in with the bundle from the store.

"Letter from home?" said Maude.

"Yeah," said Ben.

"What's it say?"

"Just a minute, Mama," said Mary Beth. She finished reading the letter and laid it on the table. "Ben," she said. "I'm sorry."

"I have to go back," he said.

"I know," said Mary Beth. "We'll miss you."

Ben was packed and ready to go by sunrise the next morning. He had said goodbye to Mary Beth inside, and she was standing in the doorway. Nellie Bell was still asleep. The night before, Ben had taken his leave of everyone else, so there was nothing left to do except to catch up and saddle his horse and ride on out. He walked to the barn with his saddle roll, and there he found Dhu Walker. Dhu's horse was saddled, and a loaded packhorse stood waiting nearby.

"What the hell are you doing?" said Ben.

"I'm going along with you," said Dhu.

"You don't have to do that."

"Can you find your own way through the Indian Territory?"

"Well, I —"

"Besides," said Dhu, "I've packed up the last of the gold. We'll stop by Drake's on the way up and unload it. Herd and Sam Ed can handle things here until we get back."

Ben looked around aimlessly, then heaved a sigh.

"All right," he said. "Let's get going."

"I'm saddled and packed," said Dhu. "I'm just waiting for you."

Chapter 2

It seemed like old times to be back out on the trail with Dhu. There were differences, of course. The war was over, and they had money in their pockets. And the biggest difference was that Ben was going back to a home without his parents where his sister was in trouble. And it wasn't really home anymore. It couldn't be home without his parents. It wouldn't seem right. He couldn't imagine the farm without them. And there was the LWM and Mary Beth and Nellie Bell and Herd and Maude and Sam Ed. The LWM was home now. Ben was flooded with emotions as he had never been before in his life, so many different emotions at once.

And there was the anxiety. He had heard that the Indian Territory was overrun with outlaws of all kinds, many of them former rebels with nothing left to them but bitterness and the vague dream of revenge and riches any way they could get them. He hadn't admitted it out loud, but he was glad to have Dhu Walker riding along with him.

They crossed the Red River where they

had laid the ambush for Old Harm and his troops — or his gang. Nearly forgotten images of bodies floating in the river returned to Ben's mind. The river was low and the crossing was easy.

"Indian Territory," said Ben.

"Choctaw Nation," said Dhu.

They rode the rest of the day without seeing anyone, then camped for the night off the trail beside a creek. They heated beans and boiled coffee over a small fire, and when they had finished eating, they settled down for the night.

"Dhu," said Ben.

"Yeah?"

"It's funny the way things works out, ain't it?"

Dhu made no response, so Ben kept on talking.

"I mean, whenever I left home — Iowa, that is — I figured that if I was to live through the war, I'd be going back home to the farm — to my folks. Things would be just like they was before."

"Things are never like they were before, Ben," said Dhu.

"Instead I got caught, and I wound up with you."

"You wound up with a wife and a little

girl, too," said Dhu.

"Yeah," said Ben. "I sure did. And a partnership in a ranch in Texas. And a lot of money. More money than I ever thought I'd see in my whole life. You know, Dhu, I didn't even like you at first."

"It showed," said Dhu.

Ben laughed.

"I guess it did," he said. His face grew long again. "Well, I'm going back now, but I ain't going back to what I thought it'd be."

"Ben, you talk too much. Get some sleep."

Dhu rolled over on his side and pulled the blanket up to his chin. The late March night was still chilly. He tried to go to sleep, but he kept thinking about Benjamin Franklin Lacey. He remembered his first impression of the man who had become one of his partners: an ignorant, white Iowa farm boy who had thought that he'd been named after a president. He wondered why, after all this time, he remained so cold toward Ben. They'd been together now for about four years. They'd ridden together, fought together, gotten rich together. Dhu supposed that in spite of everything they'd been through together, he still felt the same way he had when he had first met Ben — at least a little bit.

"Dhu?" said Ben.

"What?"

Dhu realized that his voice had come out with a hard edge, and he knew that Ben had been able to detect it, in fact, wouldn't have been able not to notice it. He was a little bit ashamed of himself for that, but he kept it to himself.

"Is it wrong what we done?" said Ben. "We come out of the war in real good shape. I mean, the war was awful and all that. A lot of people was killed and hurt. But if the war hadn't come along, we wouldn't even know each other, much less be partners. We wouldn't have our ranch. I'd never have met Mary Beth, and little Nellie Bell, well, she wouldn't even have ever been born. I — I got to say, just for my own self, I got to say I'm glad we had the war. And that don't seem right. Does it?"

Dhu thought for a long while in silence, and Ben had about decided that he wasn't going to get an answer to his question. He was almost surprised when Dhu finally did speak.

"Nothing's all good or all bad," Dhu said, "and when there's nothing you can do about things, there's no sense in worrying about them. The war wasn't your fault, Ben. You're just lucky that it brought you Mary Beth and that beautiful little girl. We're all lucky that we lived through it, and it brought us wealth. Would it be better if Old Harm had lived to get rich off that gold? That was his intention."

"No," said Ben. "Hell, no. Not him."

"Well, there you go. Now quit thinking. You're just not equipped for it."

Ben rolled over on his other side, his back toward Dhu, and jerked his blanket up close under his chin.

"That's a hell of a thing to say to me," he said. He knew that Roderick Dhu Walker, the half-breed Indian named for a character out of a storybook, was the smarter of the two with his fancy education, and Ben still resented that fact, especially when — like now — Dhu put him down. Ben tried to tell himself, as he had so many times since he had known Dhu Walker, that it wasn't his fault. He had been raised on a farm and had to work when he was growing up. But he knew that he was only trying to deceive himself with that line of talk. He had gone to school. He just hadn't liked it and had never done well at it. He grudgingly admitted to himself that the Indian really was just smarter than he.

"Damn it," he muttered out loud, but Dhu didn't hear him. Dhu was already asleep.

Katharine Lacey was bundled up against the cold March wind of southern Iowa. She had slopped the hogs, fed the chickens, and milked the cow. There was still plenty to be done, but she was cold and hungry and already tired. She figured it was nearly noon anyway, so she was headed for the house to fix herself something to eat. She would take care of that problem, rest up a bit, and then get back to work. She had almost reached the front porch when she heard the buggy approaching. She turned to look, and immediately she recognized the rig. She stood waiting, arms crossed over her bosom, until the shining carriage drawn by a sleek gray mare pulled up just in front of her.

"Whoa, there. Whoa," said the stocky, red-faced, middle-aged man holding the reins. The mare fidgeted and blew, settling down.

"Hello, Mr. Ord," said Katharine.

"Good morning, Miss Lacey," said the banker. "Can I have a few minutes of your time?"

"I was just going in the house," said Katharine. "Come on and have some coffee."

"That sounds good on a day like this," said Ord, puffing as he climbed out of his carriage to follow Katharine into the modest frame farmhouse. Inside, Katharine stoked up the fire and put water on to boil. She decided to wait until Ord was gone before starting to prepare her meal.

"Have you given any more thought to my offer?" said Ord.

"Of course I've thought about it," said Katharine, still puttering around the stove.

"Well?"

Katharine ignored the question. She got the coffee cups and saucers down from the cupboard and arranged them on a tray with a sugar bowl, cream pitcher, and spoons. She checked the water, then poured in some ground coffee. Willard Ord squirmed impatiently in the chair where he sat waiting. At long last, Katharine served the coffee.

"Thank you," said Ord. He sweetened and creamed his coffee and gave it a tentative sip to check the taste.

"So," he said, adding more sugar, "what do you think of my offer?"

"I think it's shamefully low, Mr. Ord,"

said Katharine. "It's not nearly what this place is worth. I think you're trying to take advantage of my unfortunate circumstances. That's blunt, I realize, but you did ask me what I think."

Ord nervously cleared his throat, then took another sip of his coffee.

"Miss Lacey," he said, "I'm a businessman. I have no use for your farm. I'm sorry for your situation, but I can't run a bank on sentiment. Under the circumstances, I think my offer is fair. It will pay off your indebtedness and leave you a small sum to help you get yourself resituated."

"A very small sum," said Katharine.

"What's the alternative?" asked the banker. "Will you be able to pay off the mortgage when it comes due? When that note comes due and you haven't paid it off in full, I'll be forced to foreclose on you. I'll have the farm anyway. I'm trying to be fair. I'm trying to help you."

Katharine took a sip from her cup.

"I suppose I should thank you," she said, "but I won't. I'll take my chances, Mr. Ord. I'll sell my hogs and my cattle and whatever else I can sell, and I'll try to make that payment. And if I fail, well, then I guess you'll have the farm after all, just like you said."

"Is that your last word?"

"Yes, it is," said Katharine. "Would you like some more coffee?"

For Newt Trainor the war was not over, and it would not be over until Newt Trainor was dead. Newt Trainor hated Yankees. He hated them, as he often said, "worse than I hate a nasty old stink bug." But Newt's vociferous hatred of Yankees and his frequent protestations of southern patriotism were inaccurate reflections of his actual wartime behavior. Though Newt and his gang of ruffians called themselves rebel soldiers, they had never had any official connection to the army of the Confederate States of America, and they had conducted, throughout the war, indiscriminate raids against anyone if they could see a potential profit in it for themselves. They robbed banks, stagecoaches, stores, and hapless travelers in Arkansas, Missouri, and Kansas, and then usually hurried across the border into Indian Territory, where the only law allowed to arrest them was federal law, for the local law was all Indian, and Indian law was not allowed to arrest white men.

Following Newt Trainor were five men — all young men, probably too young to vote. Their memories were not long enough to recall much besides the war. Their leader was a little older, perhaps twenty-five. The younger men admired, respected, and feared him. They followed his orders without question. And why shouldn't they? They led a life of free and wild adventure. They always had money in their pockets, and the money made it easy enough to get whiskey and women.

There was Billy Bardette, tall and lanky with long, straight, greasy hair. His major concern in life was finding boots big enough to fit his long, narrow feet. Bobby Brown was short, skinny, blond, pale, and acne-faced, but he had the watery blue eyes of a killer. There was the Kiamichi Kid, who gave a long pronunciation to the first vowel of his sobriquet. When Newt Trainor had first met him, Trainor had asked him where he came from. "The Kiamichi Mountains," the youngster had said, and Trainor had given him his new name. Red-haired Murv Maddox sat in his saddle with his back bowed. He wore two guns, and he carried them backward for a cross draw. And there was Eli Turnbull. He wore steel-rimmed glasses, and he had the look and the manner of a scholar. His saddlebags were stuffed with cheap adventure novels.

Together they had become known as the Border Rats. The name had first been applied to them by a journalist in southern Kansas, and he had certainly meant it derogatorily. But the Border Rats had liked it, and they had adopted the name enthusiastically. None of them had any aspirations in life beyond what they had already achieved. They could see nothing ahead but more of the same.

Newt Trainor hauled back the reins on his mount, and the rest of the Border Rats pulled up obediently behind him. Their horses stamped and faunched and blew. They had stopped at the crest of a hill, and below them lay a small town.

"Right there she is," said Trainor. "That's where we're going. That dinky little town has got its own bank, and all the Kansas farmers around keep their money in it."

"It's nice of them to put it all in one place for us like that," said the Kiamichi Kid.

"Yes, it is," said Trainor. "It's real nice. Now, do y'all see that brick building down there on the far side of the main street? That's the bank. We're going to ride right down there, right in front of the bank. Me and Billy and the Kid will go inside. You others will hold our horses till we get back out with the money. The other thing you'll do is you'll start shooting up the town just as soon as we get in the bank. That'll keep folks off the street. When we come back out and get mounted up, we'll all ride out together back this way, and we'll keep shooting up the town till we're plumb clear of it. Y'all got that?"

The five younger Rats all gave affirmative answers.

"Come on then," said Trainor, and they started down the hill intent on mischief.

Folks watched them as they rode down the street, some with curiosity, some with trepidation, for the Border Rats were a seedy looking bunch and were noticeably heavily armed. A few people got themselves inside the handiest door. The Rats stopped in the middle of the street in front of the bank. Three of them dismounted, looked around, and went into the bank. The three remaining on horseback pulled out revolvers and began to fire. Women and children screamed. Men shouted. Everyone ran for cover.

A man wearing a badge came running around a corner with a shotgun in his hands, and red-haired Murv dropped him in the street with one shot.

Inside the general store across the street from the bank, a toothless, gray-bearded man sat by the potbellied stove chewing tobacco and spitting.

"What's all the commotion?" he asked.

"I don't know," said the merchant as he made his way cautiously to the front window to take a peek. "It looks to me like they're robbing the bank."

"By God," said the old man, and he got up to take a look.

Across the street, inside the bank, Newt Trainor, Billy Bardette, and the Kiamichi Kid each had sacks stuffed with money.

"Let's go," said Trainor. The other two went outside, and Trainor, for no apparent reason, shot a teller in the chest before he followed them. They mounted up. All six were firing random shots. "Light out," shouted Trainor, and they all kicked their horses in the sides and headed out of town, back the way they had come from. The Kiamichi Kid was in the rear.

The front door of the general store came open a crack, and the old toothless graybeard poked a rifle through the crack, took aim, and fired. The Kid yelped and jerked, but he kept his saddle and continued riding. Soon the Border Rats were out of sight.

Chapter 3

Sam Ed McClellan had grown up big and hard and tough, and it was a good thing too. The LWM crew had so far encountered remarkably little trouble from the former rebels in the neighborhood, but there was always the potential for trouble. There was plenty of seething hostility, not only because of the polarization of the community caused by the recent war, but also because the McClellans and Ben and Dhu had killed some of the rebel sympathizers that time they had attacked the McClellan farmhouse in force. The sympathizers had brought it on themselves, but that made little if any difference to their surviving friends and relatives. Thane Savage was one of those embittered survivors.

Savage, a big, brawling, illiterate north Texas cowboy of about twenty-five years, did not know who had killed his uncle Clemson, but he did know that Clem, his favorite uncle, had been among the men who had attacked the McClellan farm, and he had been killed there in front of the McClellan house, shot off his horse by someone in the house. The old man . . . young Sam Ed . . . it didn't really matter to the mind of Thane Savage. The LWM crew had killed Uncle Clem, and Savage was filled with hatred and a burning desire for revenge. He had his cronies, too. Most of them, like Savage, worked as cowboys for Isaac Meriwether, a big rancher with a spread to the south of Preston. Meriwether had served the Confederacy as a captain of cavalry, and most folks around the neighborhood still called him Captain Meriwether out of respect for his former rank.

So it was bound to happen, and at last it did, when several members of the Meriwether crew caught Sam Ed in Preston alone one afternoon. He had just tied up in front of Elmer Tipton's general store and was about to go inside. Laughing, Thane Savage stepped out the door and was followed immediately by Charlie Bair and Hoop Roberts. When Savage saw Sam Ed, the laughter stopped abruptly. Savage stood just in front of the door. Bair stood to his right, Roberts to his left. Savage glared viciously at Sam Ed. Sam Ed glanced at the three hardcases, then stepped up onto the boardwalk.

"Excuse me," he said.

"You want to get by me," said Savage, "you got to push me out of your way."

"I got no quarrel with you, Savage," said Sam Ed. "Just let me pass."

"Yeah? Well, I got a quarrel with you. With you and that whole nest of Yankees at the LWM."

"Step aside," said Sam Ed.

"Like hell," said Savage, and he took a wide and wild swing with his big right fist at Sam Ed's jaw. Sam Ed deftly blocked the punch with his left and drove his own right into the midsection of Savage. Savage doubled over, but his two henchmen flew into action. Bair hit Sam Ed on the jaw, spinning him toward Roberts. Roberts drove a hard right into Sam Ed's face. Sam Ed staggered backward, falling off the boardwalk and landing on his back in the dirt street. Bair and Roberts were after him in a flash, kicking with their pointed boots. Sam Ed covered his head with his arms.

"Pick him up," shouted Savage. He had just caught his breath, and he was still panting and red in the face. The other two cowboys grabbed Sam Ed by his arms and hauled him up to his feet. One eye was swollen shut already, and he was bleeding from his nose and from a corner of his mouth. He shook his head, trying to clear it, and spat blood. Savage stepped up to face him.

"Your kind ain't wanted around here, McClellan," he said. "I suggest you pack up and move north while you still can."

"Make me," said Sam Ed.

Savage drove his fist into Sam Ed's belly. Sam Ed fell forward with a groan, but he was kept up on his feet by the other two cowboys.

"Damn blue-belly Yankee," said Savage. "I'll make you get out, all right. I'll make you wish you never seen Texas. I'll damn sure make you wish you never seen Thane Savage. Blue-belly Yankee."

Savage drove another fist into Sam Ed's gut, and Sam Ed sucked in a deep breath.

"That's better than being a yellow-bellied coward," he said.

Furious, Savage pounded Sam Ed with a right, a left, and another right, all to the body. Then he grabbed a handful of Sam Ed's hair in his left hand and pulled his head up. He hauled back his own right hand in order to deal a deadly blow to Sam Ed's face, but he was stopped abruptly by a harsh command from just behind him.

"Savage," the voice roared. "That's enough of that."

Savage, his fist poised, looked over his

shoulder at the commanding presence of Isaac Meriwether.

"This here son of a bitch is a McClellan," protested Savage.

"I don't care who he is, Savage. Back off," said Meriwether. "Now. And you two range bums — turn him loose."

"Captain," said Bair, his voice whiney, "he's a damn Yankee."

"Did I ask you who he was? The war is over, boys," said Meriwether. "And besides that, if you have a bone to pick with someone, try to make it an even fight. I don't ever want it said that anyone who rides for me has to fight like this. Three on one. It's disgraceful. Now turn him loose."

When Bair and Roberts released his arms, Sam Ed's knees buckled, and he almost collapsed. He struggled and managed to keep his feet though, and he daubed at the blood on his face with a sleeve.

"You three get on back to the ranch," said Meriwether.

The punchers looked at Sam Ed, then at their boss. They hesitated, Bair and Roberts looking to Savage for guidance.

"Go on," said Meriwether, "before I get mad. Get out of my sight and hope that by the time I see you next, you still have your jobs."

They turned and walked away, going toward their mounts, which were tied just down the street. Meriwether took a couple of tentative steps toward Sam Ed.

"Are you all right?" he asked.

"Yeah," said Sam Ed. "I will be. But if you hadn't have come along, they might have killed me. Thanks, Captain Meriwether."

"I have no love for Yankees, Mr. McClellan, but I do believe in a fair fight," said the captain. "If you're all right, then I'll bid you good day."

He touched the brim of his hat and turned to follow his hired hands on their way out of town. Sam Ed watched him for a moment, then staggered toward the watering trough nearby. It wasn't over. He knew that. He would just try to make sure that the next time he ran into any of those three, he wouldn't be outnumbered or caught off guard.

Ben and Dhu rode their horses up to the creek and dismounted to let the animals drink. Ben was checking the load on the packhorse, and Dhu was looking around, studying the landscape. He hadn't said anything about it, but Ben knew that Dhu was keeping a sharp eye out for possible road agents.

"Where are we?" asked Ben.

"I'm not real sure," said Dhu, "but I think we've made it to the Creek Nation."

"God, I hope we get to Katharine on time," said Ben. "What if we get up there and she's already gone?"

"Where would she be gone to?"

"I don't know. That's just what I mean. If she loses the farm and has to leave, I won't even know where to look for her. She'd just be gone."

"We'll find her," said Dhu. "Come on. Let's get going."

The Border Rats stopped running when they crossed the line into Indian Territory. If anyone was following them, they'd have to stop at the border . . . that is, if it was the law. If it wasn't the law, Newt Trainor didn't give a damn. He'd blow them away. There was an abandoned cabin in the woods that they knew about. They had used it before, and they stopped there. Newt Trainor told red-headed Murv to stay outside and watch the trail, just in case anyone from Kansas had been bold enough to follow. The Kiamichi Kid almost fell off his horse in dismounting. He stood on unsteady legs, holding onto the saddle horn to keep his feet. His shirt was blood soaked, front and back.

"Newt," he said. "I'm hurt bad. I need a doctor, Newt."

"Did you hold onto that money sack?" said Trainor.

"I got it right here, Newt," said the Kid. "I'm bleeding like a stuck pig."

Trainor walked over to the Kid. It was amazing to him how much younger he sounded, hurt and scared. He sounded like a whining baby. But that didn't make Trainor sympathetic. It disgusted him.

"Here," he said. "Let me have that sack."

The Kid let Trainor take the money sack from him, and he stood swaying dizzily, still gripping the saddle horn.

"Damn," said Trainor, looking at the bloody exit wound in the Kid's chest. "That is bad. Somebody got you for sure, Kid."

"I need a doctor real bad, Newt," said the Kid. "Will you get me to a doctor?"

"Hell no, Kid," said Trainor. "It's too goddamned late for that."

He pulled the six-gun out of his holster and fired point-blank into the heart of the Kiamichi Kid, and the Kid fell back — dead.

"Godamighty, Newt," said red-headed Murv. "You killed the Kid."

"It was the only kind-hearted thing to do, Murv," said Trainor. "You didn't want to watch the poor boy bleed to death slow, did you? Watch him suffer? Coughing and choking on blood? His tongue swelling up? His eyes bugging out? Face turning blue? Hell, boys, I'd do the same thing for any of you. And, by God, I hope you'd be as good to me."

He turned and walked into the cabin carrying two money sacks. The others stood staring at the remains of the Kiamichi Kid. At last Billy Bardette, clutching the third money sack, shrugged.

"Hell, I guess he's right," he said, and he followed Trainor into the cabin. The rest, except Murv, did the same. Murv climbed back into the saddle and began to back-track a ways to watch for any signs of pursuit.

Inside the cabin Trainor took all three sacks of money and dumped their contents into a pile on a dusty tabletop. Then he started counting.

"Look at all that money," said Billy Bardette.

"We're rich," said Bobby Brown.

"Richer by one more share, too," said Billy, a cold, sideways smile on his youthful face.

"What? Oh, you mean because of the Kid," said Eli. "Yeah. We are." He took a deep breath and sighed out loud. "That's a heap of money."

"Maybe fifty thousand dollars," said Bobby.

"I'll bet there is," said Eli. "At least fifty thousand."

Suddenly Trainor banged his fist down on the table and sprang to his feet.

"Shit," he said. "Three thousand forty-six dollars and twenty-six cents."

"What?" said Bobby.

"You heard me, damn it to hell. It's all small bills and pocket change. Those Kansas bastards outsmarted us."

"How much is it apiece?" asked Bobby.

"Hell, I don't know," said Trainor. "Figure it out. It ain't much. That's what I know."

Eli sat down at the table and took a scrap of paper and a stub of a pencil out of his pocket. He figured laboriously for a few minutes while Trainor paced the floor like a caged animal.

"Well?" said Billy.

"Six hunnerd and nine dollars and twenty-five cents each," said Eli, "with a penny left over."

"Divide it up then," said Trainor, "and

give me the goddamned penny."

Eli handed the penny to Trainor and started counting out the shares. Trainor walked outside. He strolled over to the body of the Kiamichi Kid and studied it for a moment. It already looked drained of blood and ghastly in death. Trainor flipped the penny toward the corpse.

"Here you go, Kid," he said. "Don't let anybody say you died for nothing."

Murv had walked out of the house just behind Trainor and had witnessed Trainor's little scene with the dead Kiamichi Kid, and he opened his mouth wide to release a loud guffaw. Trainor looked over his shoulder at Murv with a cold, dispassionate look. Then he smiled.

Chapter 4

Trail weary, Ben and Dhu prepared to camp on the banks of the Illinois River in the Tahlequah district of the Cherokee Nation. They had been traveling almost a week. They would sleep the night and reach the home of Nebo Drake about noon the next day. Then they would resume their trip to Iowa. Before leaving Texas they had taken plenty of traveling money out of the bank in Preston, and after their stop at Drake's place where they would sell the remainder of their somewhat ill-gotten gold, they would have even more. It would certainly pay to be cautious, and both men were well aware of that fact. The first precaution was simply to appear as inconspicuous as possible. Except for the packhorse, which was carrying the gold, Ben and Dhu appeared to be common cowboys. The packhorse was their biggest liability. It would draw attention, curiosity, and speculation. They had already agreed that once they had gotten rid of the gold, they would also leave the packhorse behind. Then they would indeed appear to be just a couple of wandering cowpokes, hardly worth any highway robber's trouble. Of course, they knew that there were plenty of cutthroats who would kill a man on the trail for his horse or saddle or even for his boots. Still, they would feel a little safer once they had unloaded the gold.

The five Border Rats were still chafing over the small amount of money they had earned by robbing the bank in Kansas as they rode on deeper into the Cherokee Nation.

"I always thought them Kansas farmers was rich," said red-haired Murv, a sulk on his face, indeed on his entire body, which rode slumped over the saddle horn.

"If they are rich," said Billy Bardette, "it's because they're too smart to put their money in the bank. They got it hid at home in a flour sack or a coffee can or something."

"Hell," said Newt Trainor, "I done told you what happened. Them bank tellers tricked us. They stuffed our sacks with small bills and pocket change so we thought we had a lot of money. We didn't hardly hurt them at all. There's a whole bunch more money in that damn bank even yet."

"Well, let's go back and get it," said Murv.

"We will," said Trainor, "but not just yet. We'll get back to them when they ain't expecting us. One of these days. We'll get the bastards."

The day was coming to an end, and Trainor was leading the Border Rats to a creek he knew was just up ahead. It would be a good place to camp for the night. Then he saw the fire.

"Hold up, boys," he said.

"What is it?" said Murv.

"Somebody's camped up there," said Trainor, "just right about where I was headed for."

"Well, hell," said Billy, "let's just go run them off."

"You all just wait right here for me," said Trainor. "I'm going down in there and look them over some. Wait right here till I get back."

They grumbled, but they stayed put while Trainor rode ahead alone.

"Rider coming," said Dhu. He stepped behind the packhorse, which had not yet been unburdened and pulled out his revolver. Ben was at the campfire boiling some coffee. Newt Trainor pulled up his mount a respectful distance from the camp.

"Hello," said Ben.

"Howdy," said Trainor. "Is that coffee?"

"Yeah," said Ben.

"Can you spare a cup? I've been on the road a spell."

"Sure," said Ben. "Climb down. We've been on the road, too."

Trainor swung down out of the saddle and walked toward the campfire.

"Where'd you ride from?" he asked.

"Texas," said Ben. "We're headed for Iowa."

"Ioway," said Trainor. "That's a far piece. What's in Ioway?"

"My family's got a farm up there."

Dhu fooled with the pack as an excuse to stay behind the packhorse. His revolver was still out and in his right hand. He didn't like the looks of their visitor, didn't like his questions, and he wished that Ben wouldn't be so loose tongued.

"My name's Charley Smith," said Trainor. "What's yours?"

"I'm Ben Lacey. My pardner over there's Dhu Walker."

Trainor looked toward Dhu, and Dhu nodded his head.

"Howdy, Walker," said Trainor. He squinted a moment. "Indian, huh?"

"I'm a Cherokee," said Dhu.

"Hell," said Trainor, "that's okay. What

the hell are two cowboys going to do on a farm in Ioway?"

"Work's work," said Dhu, "wherever you can find it."

"Yeah, I reckon," said Trainor.

Ben decided the coffee was boiled enough. He poured a cup for Trainor and handed it to him.

"Obliged," said Trainor.

Ben poured another cup and stood up, turning to walk toward Dhu, but Dhu waved him back.

"Later," he said. Ben sat back down by the fire.

"What about you?" he said to Trainor.

"Huh?"

"Where'd you ride in from, and where you going?"

"Oh. I just come from Texas," said Trainor. "Might ride up to Ioway. You never know."

"Why don't you just slug that coffee on down and ride out of here?" said Dhu.

"That ain't friendly," said Trainor.

Ben felt his face flush. He suddenly felt stupid. Dhu had ways of doing that to him. He had realized too late that there was something wrong with their visitor, something that Dhu had spotted or sensed right away. He sat still, his eyes on Trainor.

Trainor took a sip of coffee, then set the cup down on the ground beside him. Dhu raised his right hand and laid it across the pack on the horse's back. It was filled with his revolver, and the revolver was pointed at Trainor. He pulled back the hammer with his thumb.

"You're the one who's not being friendly," he said. "You ride into our camp and drink our coffee, then you ask questions that are none of your business, and you answer our questions with lies."

"What lies?"

"You didn't come from Texas, and you're not headed for Iowa, and I doubt that your name is Smith."

"Hey, wait a minute," said Trainor.

"You've had your minute," said Dhu. "Now ride out."

Trainor stood up slowly, holding his hands out away from his guns. He backed up to his horse, his eyes on Dhu, then he mounted.

"That ain't friendly," he said, and he turned his horse and rode off. Dhu watched him until he had disappeared. Then he eased down the hammer on his Colt and reholstered it.

"I guess you think I'm pretty stupid," said Ben.

"He was interested in this pack animal,"

said Dhu, ignoring Ben's comment, "and I'll bet you that he's got friends out there somewhere."

"What'll we do?"

"We can't ride on. The horses need rest. Besides, we don't know just where they are out there. We'll just have to keep watch tonight and be careful tomorrow."

They took turns sleeping, although in Ben's case it was mostly trying to sleep. As far as he could tell, Dhu slept just fine, and Ben resented it. In the morning they packed up to go, and they left their campsite without taking time for breakfast or even coffee. There was no sign of the man who had called himself Charley Smith or of anyone else.

"Maybe he just went on," said Ben.

"Maybe."

"Maybe he didn't have no buddies out there."

"Maybe."

Ben had a feeling, though, that Dhu didn't believe either one of those statements. Ben, too, was nervous.

"Dhu? You think they're out here somewhere?"

The countryside was hilly and wooded, covered with trees and brush, like most of the Cherokee Nation.

"Just ride on, Ben," said Dhu, "and keep your eyes opened."

"Goddamn Indian ordered me out of his camp," said Newt Trainor. "Likely I'll kill him for it. Indian and a Yankee. A farmer from Ioway. They're dressed like cowboys, but they're leading a loaded packhorse. I'm wondering what it is they're packing."

"I'm wondering the same thing," said Murv.

"Let's go get them," said Billy Bardette.

"We'll get them, all right," said Trainor. "But we'll ride up farther ahead and find a good spot. We'll get them by surprise. Right now they're expecting us. That Indian's sly. He's figured us out, I'll bet you. So we'll let them ride along awhile. Get relaxed. Forget about us. Then we'll get them good."

"Mama," said Sam Ed, "the sheriff won't do nothing. I'm okay. Just let it go."

"The sheriff won't do nothing," said Herd McClellan, "but by God, I will."

He went to the gun rack on the wall and pulled down his rifle.

"Put it back, Papa," said Sam Ed.

"What do you mean, 'put it back'? We ain't going to let them get away with

53

what they done to you."

"I'll get them, Papa," said Sam Ed. "I'll get them one at a time. They can't stick together everywhere they go. It might take me a little while to get it done, but I'll do it. Charlie Bair. Hoop Roberts. Thane Savage. I'll whip each one, one at a time."

"Herd?" said Maude.

Herd put the rifle back on the wall.

"The boy's right, Maude," he said. "When a boy's right over his old man, he's growed. And he's right. That's the way to do it, son."

Sam Ed's first chance came sooner than he expected. He was riding along the edge of the LWM property when he saw a lone rider coming from the direction of Colbert's Ferry. The rider was heading for Preston, and would, if left alone, ride right past Sam Ed and never notice him there. Sam Ed rode a little closer and watched. He stayed close along the edge of the thicket that grew by the river. Then he got a good look. It was Charlie Bair. Sam Ed paid out his lariat and rode toward Bair, approaching from the east, from Bair's left side. When Bair noticed the attack coming, it was already too late. The wide loop was coming at him. He ducked and reached for his revolver at the same time, but the noose snared him. Sam Ed's well-trained horse pulled the rope tight, and it pinned Bair's arms to his sides, then pulled him out of the saddle. He hit the ground hard. His six-gun flew off to one side. The wind was knocked out of his lungs.

He was sucking hard, trying to get air back into his lungs when Sam Ed stepped up close. Sam Ed picked up Bair's revolver and removed the cylinder, tossing it off to one side. Then he tossed the revolver away even farther. He unbuckled his own gun belt and walked back to his horse. There he hung the gun belt on the saddle horn and turned back to face Bair. By this time Bair had gotten his breath, and he freed himself from Sam Ed's loop.

"It's just you and me," said Sam Ed.

"Well, now," said Bair, "that's just fine and dandy."

"You got your wind back?"

"Hell, I could lick you if I had the whooping cough," said Bair.

"Come on then," said Sam Ed. "Get it on."

Bair's eyes narrowed to evil slits as he raised his fists and closed in on Sam Ed. The two young men circled each other tentatively, then Bair swung a right cross. It missed. Sam Ed jabbed twice with his left. The first connected. The second was short. Bair swung again with his right and missed again, and Sam Ed's left split Bair's lower lip. Mad, Bair charged into Sam Ed with a roar. His arms wrapped around Sam Ed and his weight and motion flung Sam Ed over backwards. He landed hard on his back with Bair on top of him. Bair flailed at Sam Ed's face with both fists.

Guarding his face with his arms, Sam Ed swung his left leg up and hooked it around Bair's head, pulling him over. Both men scrambled to their feet. Bair swung wildly, and Sam Ed's left jab caught him square on the nose. It was followed by a hard right to the jaw. Bair staggered and leaned forward, covering his face with both hands.

"I'm hurt," he said.

"You had enough?"

"Yeah. Yeah. I'm hurt."

"That's one," said Sam Ed. He turned to walk to his waiting horse. Looking back, he saw that Bair was still doubled over, still holding his face. He hesitated.

"How bad you hurt?" he asked.

"I think you broke my jaw," said Bair.

"Can you ride?"

"Yeah. I think so."

"Well, come on," said Sam Ed. "My house is the closest place we can go to. We'll look after you there."

Chapter 5

By the time they reached the LWM, poor Charlie Bair's face was swollen and puffy. And it wasn't just his jaw causing the grisly disfiguration. His nose, too, was puffy and red, and he was in pain. As Sam Ed helped him down from the saddle, Herd stepped out on the porch, shotgun in hand, followed close by Maude.

"Who's that?" said Herd.

"Oh, this here's Charlie Bair," said Sam Ed, "from over at Captain Meriwether's place."

"What happened to him?" said Maude. "He looks to be pretty bad hurt."

"Ah, we just had us a little tussle," said Sam Ed. "That's all."

"He licked me good," said Bair.

"Is this one of them three that jumped you in town?" asked Herd.

"Well, yeah," said Sam Ed. "He was."

"Well, what the hell's he doing here? Get him out of here before I shoot him," said Herd.

"Hell, Papa," said Sam Ed, "I whipped him. I ain't mad at him no more. Besides, he's hurt. He thinks I busted his jaw."

"Well, get him on inside then," said Maude. "I'll see what I can do. But you watch your tongue around my house, boy."

"Yes, ma'am," said Sam Ed, and he helped Bair up onto the porch and was on the way into the house. Charlie Bair was groaning. Maude was holding the door open. Herd started to say something in protest, but he stopped himself. Sam Ed and Maude were both against him on this. He decided that it was no use. He'd just have to go along with it.

"Damn it all to hell," he said, and he followed them inside.

They were getting close to the Arkansas border, and the hills were getting higher and steeper with each mile. It was late evening, and the day was still sultry. March was like that in the Cherokee Nation. It could be cold one day and hot the next. Violent storms with hard driving rains and pounding hail could sweep down suddenly with winds that could uproot trees. Deadly tornadoes were common in March and April, and they often came with almost no warning at all.

Dhu would rather have camped beside a stream, but the timing had not worked out.

"We can manage all right here for the night," he said.

He dismounted and started to pull the saddle off his horse. He had decided to stop there because it was the first wide spot along the trail he had seen for some time, and he didn't know how far it would be to the next one. The drop-off to their right, to the southeast, was steep and the trail was narrow. To their left, the rocky hillside rose sharply. But at this one spot there was a wide, flat area, room for a camp and grass for the horses.

Dhu had pulled off the saddle and was holding it with both hands in front of his chest when the shot rang out and the bullet thudded into the saddle leather. Ben had been just about to swing down from the back of his mount. He hesitated. Dhu dropped his saddle. His horse neighed and ran back the direction they had come from. Ben, still in the saddle, drew out his revolver and looked around for a target. Dhu pulled his gun, too. Three more shots sounded, and the bullets kicked up dust between Ben and Dhu. Dhu ran to his right to avoid the barrage, but the next shot caught him in the left shoulder, and he staggered, slipped, and fell down the steep hillside.

"Dhu!" Ben yelled, and he fired back, but he knew that he was wasting ammunition. He hadn't been able to locate their attackers. Another shot came close, and Ben turned his horse and raced it after Dhu's runaway mount.

When the Border Rats rode down the trail to the campsite, they found the packhorse calmly grazing and Dhu's saddle lying on the ground.

"We going after that one old boy?" asked Bardette.

"Hell, no," said Trainor. "Let him go. That was that Ioway farmer. He ain't nothing."

"What about the Indian then?" said Bardette. "Maybe he ain't dead."

"Well, Billy," said Trainor, "you just go on over there to the edge and find out, if you're so goddamned worried about it. Go on. Go find him."

"I'm just trying to be careful is all," said Bardette, and he rode close to where the hillside dropped off sharply. He stretched in his saddle, standing in the stirrups and leaning forward to try to see over the side. Then he dismounted and walked closer, feeling the ground with his foot before putting his weight on it. He went down a few steps, craning his neck. Trainor turned his attention toward Bobby Brown.

"Bobby, ride down the trail a little ways," he said. "Make sure that Ioway ain't trying to sneak back on us."

"If he is, I'll stop his ass," said Brown. He kicked his horse and started down the trail at a gallop. Trainor rode casually over to the packhorse. He studied it for a moment, still sitting in his saddle.

"I wonder what them old boys was packing," he said, reaching under his hat to scratch the top of his head.

"Well, let's just tear into it and find out," said Murv.

"No, hell," said Trainor. "Not yet. Just hold on a minute now. We'll find out soon enough."

He looked over toward the edge just in time to see Billy Bardette reappearing, his face white with fear.

"Damn, I like to slipped and fell off down there," said Bardette.

"What'd you see, Billy?" said Trainor.

"Not a damn thing. It's a long way down there, and I didn't see a sign of that Indian, but I damn sure like to fell down and killed myself."

"Well, he went over right there," said Murv. "I seen him go down."

"Forget about him," said Trainor. "If the shot didn't kill him the fall did."

Just then Bobby Brown came riding back up the trail.

"That Ioway's long gone, Newt," he said. "I didn't see no sign of him. He shucked it, he did. Scared to death of us, I bet."

"All right," said Trainor. "Murv, grab that packhorse, and let's get the hell out of here."

Dhu hurt all over from his tumble down the hill. He was so banged up that he didn't notice the bullet wound any more than any one of the many bruises. But mostly he was angry. He was angry at the attackers, of course, and he felt sure that they were the ones he had been expecting, the ones led by "Smith." And he was angry at himself for having let down his guard, for having let himself get taken so easily. He had relaxed some, thinking that they had traveled far enough since their original meeting with Smith to be safe. Obviously, he had been wrong. And then he was angry at Ben, too. Why? For the same reasons he was angry at himself.

He groaned and lifted his head. The hillside spun around him, and he eased it back down. Slowly, he lifted his right arm and let it down again. Then he lifted the left, and a sharp pain raced through the arm and shoulder reminding him of the bullet wound.

"Ah."

He groaned out loud as he eased the arm back down, and he took a couple of deep breaths. Then he turned his head to look at the shoulder. The wound was ugly, but he didn't think that it was serious, especially if he could manage to get it tended to soon, get the bleeding stopped, and get it wrapped up. He lifted one leg and then the other, bending the knees as he did. He didn't think that anything was broken. He would just have to wait for his head to quit spinning before he tried to get up. That's all. And he wondered just where the hell Ben Lacey was and what had happened to him.

Ben had ridden back down the trail to the first sharp bend. There he had lurked behind a boulder waiting for pursuit. None came. He waited until he felt reasonably sure that no one was after him. Then he rode slowly and cautiously back out onto the trail and back toward the bend. He held a revolver in his right hand, and he looked up the trail toward the campsite.

The trail was clear for as far as he could see, but he couldn't see all the way to the campsite. They might still be there — whoever they were. He wondered if Dhu had been right about Smith when he had said that Smith wasn't alone, that he had been checking them over and would be back later with his friends, and he wondered if it was Smith and his friends who had attacked them.

He had to find Dhu, but he couldn't go back to the campsite not knowing whether or not the attackers were still there. He wondered if he could locate Dhu by riding off the trail and down along the bottom of the hill. He had seen Dhu fall, but he had only seen him out of the corner of his eye. He had been too busy dodging bullets and trying to locate their attackers. He assumed that Dhu had been hit, but he didn't have any idea how badly he might be hurt, or how far down the hill he might have fallen.

He clucked and urged his horse off the trail, going down the hillside, and as he rode, he wondered if Dhu was lying hurt somewhere thinking that he had run out on him. And there was yet another reason for urgency. The sun had already dropped down below the western treeline and the sky was getting dark. If he didn't find Dhu soon, it would be too dark to search until morning, and Ben didn't know whether or not Dhu could stand to wait that long.

The Border Rats stopped again. They were outside the walls of an old stone farmhouse. The roof had long since fallen in, and the windows and doors were missing, but the giraffe-skin patterned stone walls stood as solid as ever. The outlaws all dismounted.

"Build us a fire, Bobby," said Trainor. "Murv, rip open that pack. Let's see what the hell we got."

Murv grinned, pulled a long knife out of his boot, and stepped over to the packhorse. He cut the ropes that held the pack in place, allowing the whole thing to fall to the ground. The packhorse whinnied and danced to the side. Then Murv dropped to his knees and started slicing canvas. He tossed aside pieces of clothing and sacks and tins of food. Then he found a leather pouch. He grabbed it and gave a heave, but it hardly budged.

"Damn," he said. "That's heavy."

Trainor ran over and shoved Murv aside. Murv fell back heavily on his backside in a sitting position. He watched from there as

Trainor reached for the pouch with both hands and lifted it, with a grunt, out of the mess that had been the pack and, turning, dropped it on the ground between his feet. He tore open the pouch, reached inside, and felt something hard and smooth and cold. He dragged it out.

"Is that gold?" said Murv, scampering up onto his hands and knees and crawling closer for a better look.

"That's gold," said Trainor. "Yes, indeed, it's gold, and there's more of them in there, boys. Gold bars."

"Hot damn," said Murv.

"Now where the hell you reckon that Indian and that Ioway got all them gold bars?" said Turnbull.

"It don't make a damn no more where they got them," said Trainor. "What matters is that we got them now."

Ben was worried. It would be dark soon. To his left, the hillside above was covered with brush and boulders and on his right was thick woods. Looking up, he couldn't quite identify the place from which Dhu had fallen. He was afraid he'd have to ride all the way back around and back up the trail to the campsite, then come down from there. But he didn't know how long Dhu

66

could afford to wait. He decided to take a risk.

"Dhu," he called out. "Dhu. Can you hear me?"

He sat quietly for a moment, listening, hoping for a reply, then he rode on a little farther.

"Up here, Ben."

Ben looked up and to his left, and he saw Dhu pulling himself up from behind a big rock. He swung down out of the saddle and hurried up to help.

"Dhu," he said, "take it easy. How bad is it?"

"I don't know," said Dhu. "I hurt all over, but I think that's mostly from the fall."

He tried to stand up, but he was woozy, so he sat down on the rock. Ben was there looking at the shoulder wound.

"We got to do something about this," he said. "Just tie it up," said Dhu. "Middle Striker's house is not far from us here. We'll go there."

Chapter 6

"Newt?" said Bobby Brown. "What do we do with it? I mean, we can't toss one of these things on a bar and get change. Can we?"

"We can take them to a bank or something and cash them in," said Billy Bardette.

"You dumb asses," said Murv. "Someone'd be wanting to know where we got gold bars. Somebody's likely to be already looking for these things."

"Well, where did them two cowboys get them?" said Billy.

"They probably stole them," said Murv. "Hell, they's thieves everywhere these days."

Eli Turnbull laughed a shrill laugh.

"Boy," he said, "you can say that again."

"So what do we do?" asked Bobby, irritated at the levity and wanting a serious answer to his serious question.

They all looked toward Newt Trainor who was just sitting and staring at the gold bars and had not spoken. He sat in silence for another moment before speaking.

"I don't know," he said. "It's the

damnedest thing. Here we got more money than I ever thought I'd see, and we can't spend it. I'm going to have to think on this."

"Couldn't we bust it up into nuggets?" asked Billy.

"Or melt it down?" said Bobby.

"No, hell," said Murv. "It's pure gold. Anyone'd know it wasn't nuggets. It's a good thing old Newt's here. You dumb kids would wind up in the pen for sure. Either that or get hung."

"Murv's right," said Trainor, shaking his head sadly. "I've got to think on this considerable."

Ben had almost forgotten what it had been like to be in the home of Middle Striker, a full-blood Cherokee who did not speak English. Following their escape from Confederate forces, he and Dhu had sought refuge there, and Ben had been nervous and afraid. He was no longer afraid or mistrustful of Middle Striker, but he did feel self-conscious and out of place. Dhu was asleep. His shoulder had been cleaned, doctored, and bandaged by Middle Striker, so Ben was, in effect, alone with the full-blood. He sat by himself outside, staring into the deep woods of the eastern Cherokee Nation.

He looked over his shoulder when he heard the sound of the door opening, and he saw Middle Striker step out. The Indian held a tin cup in his hand. Steam rose from the cup in little wisps that quickly dissipated into the cool spring air.

"Kawi jaduli?" said Middle Striker.

Ben opened his mouth as if to speak, but of course he had no idea what to say.

"Uh."

Middle Striker held the cup out toward Ben with a questioning look on his face, and Ben realized that Middle Striker had probably been offering it to him.

"Oh," said Ben. "Yeah. Yes. Thanks."

He reached for the cup and took it. It was full of fresh, hot coffee. He sipped from the cup, burning his lips and tongue just a bit, and he smiled self-consciously and looked up at Middle Striker.

"It's good," he said. "Thank you," and he nodded his head. God, he felt stupid. Middle Striker smiled, nodded, and went back in the house. Ben wondered why he should feel stupid not being able to understand the Cherokee language. Middle Striker couldn't understand English. But then Dhu Walker could understand and speak both languages. It was always Dhu that made Ben feel stupid. It was always Dhu.

Ben wasn't worried about Dhu. The wound wasn't a serious one, and it had gotten attention soon enough. Dhu had assured Ben on their way to Middle Striker's house that Middle Striker was particularly skillful at dealing with gunshot wounds. He wasn't worried about Dhu, but he was worried. Katharine was in trouble in Iowa, and Ben felt an urgent need to get to her as soon as possible. He wondered how long it would be before Dhu was ready again to travel. How much time would have been wasted? He wondered if he should go ahead alone, but he wasn't at all sure that he could even find his way without Dhu, and what if he ran into more outlaws along the way?

Then there was the gold. The gold wasn't as important as Katharine's problem, but it was important. He knew that Dhu would be anxious to pursue the thieves, the men who had ambushed them, shot Dhu, and stolen their packhorse. By now, he thought, they would have discovered the gold. He wondered if it had been the man who called himself Smith at their camp that night. He suspected that it had been. After all, Dhu suspected him, and

Dhu was usually right.

Ben wanted to go after them, too. It wasn't the gold so much. It was more. The man had been a guest at their camp. Then he and others had fired from ambush without warning. They had shot Dhu and might easily have killed both Dhu and Ben. Then they had stolen from them. And Ben wanted his revenge. But Katharine needed him, and now Dhu was hurt, and time was wasting.

Ben slurped at the hot coffee. It tasted good. There was a cool breeze blowing through the woods. Some of the trees were beginning to show green, and here and there were patches of green on the ground. It would have been pleasant sitting there in that quiet setting had he not had urgent business to attend to, had he not been anxious about the gold, angry at the outlaws, worried about his sister, and, yes, he admitted to himself, worried at least a little about Dhu.

He finished the coffee and stood up to take the cup back inside, and he saw Middle Striker sitting in a straight-backed, cane-bottomed chair beside the bed in which Dhu rested. Dhu and Middle Striker were talking low in Cherokee. Ben felt his face burn, and for an instant he felt again the old sensation that he was being talked about. He reminded himself that Middle Striker spoke no English. The only way Dhu and Middle Striker could communicate with each other was in Cherokee. He's probably asking Dhu how his shoulder feels, Ben told himself. Still, he felt self-conscious.

He put the cup on the table and stepped across the room to stand just behind Middle Striker and slightly to his left. He looked down at Dhu.

"How you feeling?" he asked.

"It still hurts a little," said Dhu, "but I'm all right. Mostly it's just throbbing now. I figure we'll head out in the morning."

"Head where?" said Ben.

"Head on to Iowa. Where else?"

"I was thinking about those men who got our packhorse," said Ben.

"We're not hurting for money, Ben," said Dhu. "It rankles to have it stolen from us, and when a man shoots me, something makes me want to get even, but your sister is up there alone in need of help."

"You're right. I was hoping you'd feel that way," said Ben. "I guess we can just write off that gold. It'll be long gone by the time we get back through here."

"We know who to look for though," said Dhu.

"We do? How?"

"I told Middle Striker about that Smith. He said Smith sounds like a man called Newt Trainor. He has a gang of outlaws who operate all around the borders of the Nations. They rob a bank in Kansas or Arkansas and then run into Indian Territory, into the Cherokee Nation or the Creek Nation. The law from Kansas or from Arkansas can't chase them in here, and the Indian law can't touch them."

"You mean they're just free in here?" said Ben, incredulous. "They can just do anything they like and get away with it?"

"The federal marshals can come after them," said Dhu, "but no one else."

"What was his name?"

"Trainor," said Dhu. "Newt Trainor. He and his gang are called the Border Rats."

"The Border Rats, huh?" said Ben.

"Border Rats," said Middle Striker, pronouncing the English words with some difficulty and nodding his head in agreement.

"Sounds like a good name for them," said Ben. "You sure you're going to feel like riding out of here in the morning?"

"If I don't, I'll let you know," said Dhu,

"but I expect I'll be ready. We've wasted enough time here as it is."

Katharine hitched a horse to the buggy; then she threw a saddle on another horse. She tied the reins of the saddle horse to the rear of the buggy and climbed onto the buggy seat to drive into town. It wasn't a long drive, but it gave her plenty of time to think, perhaps too much time. She couldn't figure out any way to come up with the cash she would need to pay off the mortgage to Ord in time to save her farm. Even if she could get the money, she couldn't see how she'd be able to make a living. She just couldn't run the farm alone. Her greatest hope was that she would somehow be able to pay off the mortgage on time and then sell the farm at a fair price. If she could manage that, she'd be able to use the money from the sale to relocate. But relocate where? She had no idea. But then, she told herself, what difference did it make? She just didn't have the mortgage money, and Ord had already made it clear that he would not extend the note.

"Not one more day," he had said.

She thought about the letter she'd received from her brother Ben after so long a time and the answer she had sent him. And she felt just a little guilty that she had mentioned her problems. She shouldn't have worried him, she thought. Then she decided that while she was in town, she'd write him another letter and tell him that everything was all right, that she had figured out how to resolve her problems. It would be a lie, but it would only be a white lie, and it would serve a good purpose. It would set his mind at ease.

Ben had his own life and a new family to worry about. She didn't have any right to be imposing her problems on him, especially when there was nothing he could do to help. He was so far away. Texas. It sounded to Katharine like the other side of the world. Like another world. Where was Texas? Somewhere far to the south. It was some mysterious place, a huge wilderness full of wild, romantic adventure. She had never really thought of Texas as being a real place at all, not until she had received the letter from Ben telling her that he was on a Texas ranch.

She wondered about Ben's wife and his daughter, and she longed to see her niece. Nellie Bell. Would she look like Ben or Mary Beth? Or, she wondered, might Nellie Bell look like her Aunt Katharine?

She might. She had seen children who favored aunts or uncles often enough. The thought intrigued her, and she wondered if she could find a way to sell the farm and come up with enough extra cash to pay her way to Texas. Preston, Texas. She would really like to see that little girl.

Then she found herself in town in front of the livery stable, and she stopped the buggy. Mr. Campbell stepped out to greet her.

"Good morning, Miss Lacey," he said. "You're in town right early today."

"Yes, Mr. Campbell," she said, climbing down from the buggy. "I wonder if I might interest you in this rig."

"You want to sell your buggy?" said Campbell.

"Yes, and the horse with it."

"What about the saddle horse?"

"I need him to get back home on, Mr. Campbell."

Campbell stepped over to the buggy. He walked around it slowly, inspecting every part. He looked the horse over as carefully.

"Come on inside, Miss Lacey," he said. "Let's see if we can come to terms."

Katharine followed Campbell inside to his office, and in a few minutes came back out. She was satisfied. She had enough to pay her bill at the general store with a small amount left over. She would have nothing left to clear up but the business of the mortgage, and that relieved her mind a little. She untied the saddle horse and, leading him along, began walking toward the general store. While she was there, she thought, she could write her letter to Ben.

Chapter 7

Ben never did figure it out, but somehow word spread through the hills that he and Dhu were there at Middle Striker's house, and soon people were showing up to visit. Ben recognized most of them from the time he had spent there during the war, just after he and Dhu had escaped from the rebels. Ben surprised himself by feeling relieved with the additional company. He recalled that he had been extremely nervous at being the only white man among a bunch of Indians the first time. But his relief had to do with the fact that some of these people could speak English, and he realized after a short while that, because of his presence there, they did speak English. Of course, they repeated everything they said in Cherokee so that Middle Striker and some of the others who could not understand English would know what had been said. In other words, they were polite to everyone. No one was left out. Ben tried to recall if they had done that the other time, but he couldn't remember. He realized, too, that even if they had done so, he wouldn't have noticed it back then.

Ready Ballard was the first one to show up. Ballard had been their original host in the Cherokee Nation, and he seemed genuinely pleased to renew his acquaintance with Ben. Ben kept thinking about how wrong he had been about these people when he first met them. And Ketch Barnett came. He, too, was real friendly.

That evening, they were sitting around talking and drinking coffee. The talk was idle chatter at first. Then it turned to catching up on news. The Cherokees learned about the ranch in Texas, and they were pleased at their friends' good fortune.

"So what brings you back up this way?" asked Barnett.

"Ben's got to go home to Iowa," said Dhu. "His sister's alone up there on the family farm and needs some help settling things. We also had a little more business to do with Nebo Drake."

The others knew about Drake. They just nodded their heads knowingly.

"But you got shot," said Ballard.

"Ambushed and robbed," said Dhu. "From what Middle Striker told me, it was Newt Trainor and the Border Rats."

"You going after them?" asked Ballard.

"Not just yet," said Dhu. "We figure that Ben's sister's problems are more urgent.

We'll go on up there and take care of business, and then we'll track those Border Rats on our way back through."

Ready Ballard spoke to Middle Striker in Cherokee for a couple of minutes, and everyone else sat quietly waiting. Occasionally Dhu nodded his head in agreement with what Ballard was saying. Middle Striker listened carefully until Ballard was finished. Then he made a brief response.

"*Wado, ginali,*" said Dhu. Then he looked at Ben. "Middle Striker says that when we come back through, we should come here first. He says that he and the others will do some scouting for us while we're gone. They just might have those Border Rats pinned down for us by then."

"Great," said Ben. "It would sure be a help. I got to admit, it sure hurts to think about just riding on and leaving them be."

"We'll get them," said Dhu, and Ben saw something almost frightening in Dhu's eyes, something that said there was no doubt that Dhu meant what he said, something that almost said, "It will happen." A moment of silence fell over the room.

"So what's been happening around here?" Dhu asked, abruptly changing the subject.

"Middle Striker's a daddy again," said Ballard.

"Again?" said Dhu. "How many does that make?" He repeated his question in Cherokee, and the Cherokees all laughed. Middle Striker gave a one-word response while grinning and ducking his head.

"Eight?" said Dhu. "Well, where are they?"

"They all went to his mother-in-law for a few days," said Ballard.

"That's why he's so relaxed," said Barnett, and again they all laughed. Ben joined in on the good-natured laughter, and he realized that he was beginning to feel comfortable with these people. Middle Striker went to get the coffee off the stove to refill the cups, and again there was a lull in the conversation. At last Ready Ballard broke the silence.

"Have you heard about our new treaty?" he said.

"No," said Dhu. "I haven't heard anything about a new treaty. Tell me."

"They said that we had to sign a new treaty with the United States after the war," said Ballard. "They said that we had been at war with them, and to end the war, we had to sign a treaty. They said that we always have to end a war with a treaty."

"But it wasn't our war," said Dhu. "We got dragged into it. It was their own war. John Ross begged them to send troops down here to keep us out of the war. And they were obligated to do that by the last treaty."

"We all know that," said Ballard, "but they seem to have forgotten. All they said was that we had joined the Confederacy, so we had to sign this new treaty."

"Damn them," said Dhu.

"Ha!" said Ketch Barnett. "It's a good thing you know English, so you can talk like that when you need to."

"So what's in this new treaty?" asked Dhu.

Middle Striker was pouring coffee all around, and Ketch Barnett started talking Cherokee. Ben figured that Barnett was just letting Middle Striker know what the discussion was all about. Middle Striker nodded his head, finished pouring the coffee, and took the pot back to the stove. Then Ballard started to answer Dhu's question.

"Well," he said, "they took some land."

"They always do," said Barnett.

"What land?" asked Dhu.

"I'm not sure," said Ballard. "Some-where up north."

"Wait a minute," said Ben. "They took away some of your land? What for?"

"Because they said we fought against them," said Barnett.

"Because you joined the Confederacy?"

"Yeah," said Barnett. "But we didn't, really."

"I know," said Ben, "but that was the reason they gave?"

"That was the reason for the whole treaty," said Ballard.

"But they didn't take land away from any of the Confederate states," said Ben.

"No," said Dhu. "They're not Indian tribes."

"Damn," said Ben. "It don't seem fair."

"Well, you're beginning to see how your government deals with Indians," said Dhu. He turned toward Ballard. "What else is in that new treaty, Ready?" he asked.

"We had to let the railroad come through," said Ballard. "Going from north to south. From Kansas to Texas. Right through the Cherokee Nation."

"Chief Ross fought against that for years," said Dhu. "Now they got their way."

"They've got a U.S. district court," Ballard continued, "and they're giving it jurisdiction over all of the Indian Territory.

The only cases our courts can hear any more are cases involving just Cherokees."

"That's why the Border Rats are safer in here than outside," said Ben.

"That's right," said Dhu. "The Border Rats and others like them."

"How are we supposed to maintain law and order in our own country," said Barnett, "when the U.S. government won't let us arrest outlaws who come in from outside?"

"Maybe they don't want us to maintain law and order," said Ballard. "One of these days, you wait and see, they're going to take the whole thing away from us, and one of their excuses for it is going to be that we can't maintain law and order. Wait and see if I'm not right about that."

"All the freed slaves are full citizens now," said Barnett.

"Of the United States?" asked Ben.

"No," said Barnett. "Of the Cherokee Nation."

"And," said Ballard, "we have a new inter-tribal council. A kind of a government of the Indian Territory. Each tribe has to send a representative to that territorial government. There's more, but that's all I can remember right now. That's the most important part anyway, I think."

"It's pretty bad," said Dhu. "It seems like each new treaty is worse than the last one."

"Well, what can you do about it?" asked Ben.

"Nothing," said Ballard. "The time is long past when we could go to war against the United States. All we can do now is just take it."

Ben felt a little bit guilty. It was, after all, his government that was doing these things to the Cherokees. It occurred to him for the first time that perhaps Dhu had good reason for being so short with him at times, that Dhu Walker and any other Cherokee had good reason to hate the United States government and the white people that it represented. But Dhu was half white himself. Ben felt confused.

"It ain't right," he said, "and I'm ashamed of my government for what it's doing here. I wish there was something I could do about it."

Later in the evening Ben found himself alone in the house with Dhu. Ready Ballard and Ketch Barnett had gone home, and Middle Striker was outside splitting logs.

"Dhu," said Ben.

"Yeah?"

"How you feeling?"

"Not too bad."

"You going to feel like riding in the morning?"

"I think so."

"Dhu?"

There was a moment of silence.

"What?" said Dhu.

"Do you hate me?"

Dhu laughed, and Ben felt his face flush.

"What kind of a fool question is that?" said Dhu. "Why would I hate you? You're my partner. Would I have a man for a partner if I hated him?"

"But I'm a white man, and it's my government that's doing all them wrong things to your people. And sometimes I think you act like you hate me."

"I don't hate you, Ben," said Dhu. He sat up straighter in the bed, and he groaned as a sharp pain shot through his side from the shoulder wound. "I wouldn't be riding to Iowa with you if I hated you. I get a little impatient sometimes, I guess. I shouldn't. Don't let me get you down, Ben. When I step out of line with you, just tell me to back off. Okay?"

Ben didn't answer, and Dhu sat quietly for a moment, thinking of what to say next.

"I don't suppose I hate anyone or anything anymore, Ben. I don't even hate the government. I used up all my hate on Old Harm, I guess. When that was all over, and I looked at Old Harm lying there dead in the dirt, looking all useless and — meaningless — all I could think of was how much I had hated the man and how much a waste that had been. Hate's not healthy, Ben. I don't hate anyone. Especially not you."

Ben thought that he hadn't heard Dhu talk so much in all the years they had been together, and when Dhu finally quit, Ben wasn't quite sure what he had said. And he still felt guilty.

Then the door opened, and Middle Striker came back into the room. He had an armload of split logs which he dropped to the floor beside the stove. Then he headed back outside.

"Ask him where he's going, Dhu," said Ben.

Dhu spoke to Middle Striker in Cherokee, and Middle Striker gave a short response.

"He's going out to split some more wood," said Dhu.

"Tell him I'm going along to help, would you?" said Ben, and he stood up to follow Middle Striker out the door. Dhu spoke to

Middle Striker, and Middle Striker smiled and nodded. Dhu watched them leave the house together. The farm boy from Iowa had learned a lot in a few short years, he thought. And he thought that he had been pretty rough on Ben. He would try to be more careful in the future, try not to be so short with Ben, so critical. Ben had been a good friend. And a good partner. Dhu decided that he would try to start treating him more like both.

Then he thought that he could almost hear his father's voice telling him, "The world's a bad enough place to live as it is, Dhu, boy. Treat people the best way you can. It doesn't cost anything to be nice to people. It's a real cheap way to make a better world. And it comes back to you. Always try to think the best of people and treat them accordingly. If they give you reason to think otherwise, that's time enough to change your approach. Not in general. Just to the individual who gave you cause. But whatever you do, don't make the world a worse place than it was when you came into it. If you have to leave a mark behind you, make it a good one."

Ben deserves better from me, Dhu thought. He's a good enough fellow. Just a little ignorant sometimes. That's all.

Chapter 8

Katharine had written her letter. Silent and alone, she stood at the counter in the store for a moment and reread what she had written.

Dear Brother,

I am so ashamed of myself for my last letter to you. I can't imagine how I must have worried you. I don't know what I must have been thinking, or maybe I wasn't thinking at all. Everything is going to be all right here. Please don't worry.

There's nothing new for me to tell you it's so soon since last I wrote. I just don't want you to be worrying. Give my love to Mary Beth and hug Nellie Bell and kiss her for her Aunt Katharine.

Love,
Katharine

She couldn't think of anything more to say, so she folded the letter and prepared it for the mail, hoping that it would set Ben's mind at ease. She wished that she could set her own mind at ease so simply. Well, at least she could pay her bill at the store. Once that was done, she wouldn't owe anyone any money except for the bank, and that would be resolved one way or another before much longer. If Ord should foreclose on her, at least she would be out of debt. She wouldn't have any money, but she would be out of debt. Maybe, she thought, she was being a fool for refusing Ord's offer. Well, then she would just be a fool. She would not, of her own choice, sell out to the greedy banker for less than what the farm was worth. She mailed her letter, paid her bill, and left the store. Back out on the street, she mounted her saddle horse and started to ride back toward the farm.

Then she stopped abruptly, confusing the poor animal. She steadied him, then thought to herself for a moment. She hadn't even tried to sell the farm. There might be another interested buyer out there somewhere, one who would give her a fair price. But how would she find out? She didn't know. Oh, how she wished she had paid more attention to the way her Daddy had done business when she still had the opportunity. He would have known how to look for a buyer. She didn't.

"Of course," she said out loud. The horse whickered and shook his head as if he thought that she had given him some command that he had not understood. "The realty agent."

Katharine had grown up on the farm. She had never had any dealings with realty agents in her life. Even so, she felt a bit foolish for not having thought of that option earlier. She turned her horse around and rode down the street to where Calvin Hellman's realty office was located. She dismounted there and tied the horse to the hitch rail. Then she pulled herself up straight, took a deep breath, and went inside.

Hellman looked up from behind his desk. He was a small man, bald, and wore steel-rimmed glasses.

"Why, Miss Lacey," he said. "What a surprise. What brings you here?"

"I'd like to sell my farm, Mr. Hellman," said Katharine. "Can you help me?"

"Why, uh, I don't know," said Hellman. "I'm not sure."

"That's your business, isn't it? Selling property for people?"

"Yes. Of course it is. But, uh, farms aren't moving so well just now. It isn't always that easy to find the right buyer just when you want one. Of course, I'll try. I can list it for you and see what happens."

"Please do that, Mr. Hellman. You see, since I'm alone now, I can't very well take care of the farm, and I have a mortgage coming due soon. If I don't sell the farm before the mortgage comes due, I'll simply lose it and have nothing."

"Of course, it's none of my business, Miss Lacey," said Hellman, "but I understood that, uh, Mr. Ord made you an offer for the farm."

"He did, Mr. Hellman. Not a very good one, though."

"Would his offer clear the mortgage?"

"Yes, it would, with just a little left over," said Katharine, "but it's still not what the farm is worth."

"I see. Um, well now. There aren't very many people around here likely to try to outbid Mr. Ord. You know that, don't you? And property, you see, that is, the value of property is determined, at least partly, that is, by what someone is willing to pay for it. Do you understand?"

"Yes," said Katharine, "I believe I do. Well, I suppose I can't hold out much hope for what you might do for me, but will you list the property for me? I do not intend to sell it to Mr. Ord for his current offer."

"Yes," said Hellman. "I see. Well. Of course, there's no guarantee, but let's just get the paperwork done here, and let's see what I might be able to do for you. All right?"

Katharine felt herself burning with rage. So the businessmen would all stick together, would they? If Willard Ord made her an insulting offer, Calvin Hellman wasn't about to try to get her a better one. He didn't want to risk getting on the bad side of Ord. So they would all gang up on a young woman alone. They were just a bunch of grown-up schoolyard bullies, she decided. To hell with them all then. She stood up abruptly.

"Never mind, Mr. Hellman," she said. "I believe that I can see right through you. Good day."

Charlie Bair's jaw hurt like the dickens, but Maude McClellan had told him that she didn't think that it was actually broken. Cracked at worst, she had said. But if Charlie tried to open his mouth, terrible pains shot all through his head. Maude and Mary Beth fed him broth so that he wouldn't have to open his mouth wide and wouldn't have to chew. Maude insisted that he stay at the McClellan house until his jaw got better. Charlie didn't understand that at first. After all, he and two other cowboys had jumped her boy, Sam Ed, in the street in Preston and proceeded to try their best to beat him into a pulp. And they would probably have succeeded, too, had not their boss, Meriwether, happened along before things had gone too far.

But soon Charlie began to understand, and the explanation was simple. The McClellans were just good people. The first indication Charlie had was when Sam Ed had taken him home after having beaten him up out on the prairie. Sam Ed had wanted his revenge, and he had gotten it. But once the fight was over, Sam Ed didn't have the heart to leave a hurt man alone. And in just the same way, Maude didn't have the heart to send a hurt man away, even if he had fought with her son. Charlie was learning a lot about human nature. Thane Savage said that the McClellans were Yankees and that all Yankees were no damn good. But Charlie Bair was learning that it just wasn't so.

He was sitting in an easy chair in the living room of the McClellan house when Sam Ed walked in.

"How you feeling, Charlie?" said Sam Ed.

"Oh, not too bad, I guess," said Charlie, keeping his teeth clenched and talking by just moving his lips. "I guess I could get up and get out of here. I feel kind of like I'm just in the way here. Sam Ed, you and your folks have been good to me. I'm kind of ashamed of what I done to you now."

"Forget it, Charlie," said Sam Ed. "Hell, let's just say we're even now and let it go at that. Okay?"

"Well, as far as the fighting's concerned, I guess we could say that, but now I'm beholden to y'all for your kindness."

"Don't worry about it, and don't be in too big a hurry to get out of here. Make sure you're all right first. Anyway, you ain't no trouble around here. Mama always cooks too much for us to eat, and we got plenty of room."

"Thanks, Sam Ed," said Charlie. "But you know, I've got a job, and the boss don't know where I've been. If I don't get back and tell him, I won't likely have a job much longer. Maybe I've already done been fired."

Sam Ed rubbed his chin and thought for a moment.

"Tell you what," he said. "I'll ride over

to Meriwether's and tell him where you're at. Tell him you been hurt, and you're healing up, and you'll be back to work just as soon as you're able. How's that?"

"Well," said Charlie, "if you want to do that for me, I'd be real grateful. I do need the job. Thanks, Sam Ed. You know, buddy, I don't know how I could ever have had a man pegged so wrong as I did you."

"Ah, shut up," said Sam Ed. "I'll head over there right now." He put his hat back on his head and went out the door.

An hour or so later, Sam Ed rode up to the big ranch house on the Meriwether spread. From a corral off to Sam Ed's right, Thane Savage came walking toward him. As he walked, he pulled out his six-gun.

"You got a lot of nerve riding in here," Savage said.

"I come to see your boss," said Sam Ed, "not you."

"You just turn around and ride back out of here," said Savage, "while you still can. I ought to blow you right out of your saddle, and I just might decide to do that, too."

Just then three more cowboys came walking from the corral to join Savage. One of them was Hoop Roberts, the third man of the team that had attacked Sam Ed in Preston that day.

"What the hell's he doing here?" said Roberts.

"It don't make no difference," said Savage. "He ain't staying."

"I come to see Captain Meriwether," said Sam Ed, "and I aim to."

The front door of the big house opened, and Meriwether himself came out onto the porch. He stood for a moment surveying the scene there before him. He recognized Sam Ed, and he recalled the fight in Preston. Two of the three men who had attacked Sam Ed in town that day were standing there with drawn six-guns.

"What's going on here?" he demanded.

"I came to see you, Captain Meriwether," said Sam Ed. "I ain't looking for no trouble."

"Put your guns away, Thane, Roberts," said Meriwether, "and get back to work. All of you."

Savage hesitated, disgruntled, then shoved the gun back into its holster. He turned sulkily and headed back toward the corral. The others followed him, but they didn't go back to work. They leaned against the fence and glared at Sam Ed and their boss.

"Now, McClellan," said Meriwether. "What's this all about?"

"I met up with Charlie Bair out on the prairie a couple of days ago," said Sam Ed, "and I whipped him for what he done to me in town. You remember."

"Yes, I remember. So, did you come here to gloat over your triumph?"

"No, sir," said Sam Ed, "that ain't why I'm here. I come over here to give you a message for Charlie."

"All right," said the captain, "I'm listening."

"Well, I guess I hurt him some, and so I took him home to my ma, and she took care of him. He's still there kind of recuperating. He was worried you'd fire him, so I told him I'd come over here and let you know how things were. He'll get back over here to work just as soon as he can."

Meriwether looked with curiosity at Sam Ed. It was a peculiar story, yet he believed it. He had no reason not to.

"That's it?" he said.

"Yes, sir. Well, I told you. That's what I said I'd do. Can I tell him he's still got a job when he gets to feeling better?"

"No," said Meriwether. "I'm sorry, but when he didn't show up, I replaced him.

99

I'm sorry he's hurt, but he brought it on himself. I've got to be able to depend on my hands. Thanks anyway for riding over."

"But Captain Meriwether," said Sam Ed, "it really ain't Charlie's fault that he got hurt. I mean, I guess it was really my fault, and I hate to cost a man his job. I like to near broke his jaw, and he just couldn't ride on over here like that. He had to heal up some, you know? Could you maybe change your mind?"

"I'm sorry, young man," said the captain, "but the decision has already been made."

Sam Ed sighed, then turned his horse to ride away. Then he stopped and looked back over his shoulder.

"Oh, yeah," he said. "I might as well go ahead and tell you long as I'm here. I intend to whip them other two first chance I get."

"I figured you would," said the captain, and he turned and went back in his house.

As Sam Ed headed back toward the LWM he felt a strange kind of satisfaction. He had failed at his mission, but he really didn't care. He had gotten to know Charlie Bair, and he liked him. He really didn't like to think of his new friend back at

Meriwether's hanging around the likes of Thane Savage again. No. He would much rather, he decided, have Charlie stay around the LWM.

Chapter 9

Billy Bardette stepped inside the bank, quickly moved to his right, and pulled out a revolver. Almost immediately, Murv Maddox, his red hair wild on his head, stepped in and to the left. He executed his cross draw and leveled two revolvers. Then Newt Trainor stepped in to stand between the two.

"Everybody stand still," he ordered. "This is a holdup."

There were three customers in the bank, one farmer, one young man in a business suit, and one middle-aged woman. Three bank employees were behind the counter: one young man, a young woman, and an older man with a slick, shiny bald head.

"Oh, no," said the slick head. "Not again. You were just here."

"That's right," said Trainor, "and you bastards tricked us. You filled up our money bags with small bills. You ain't going to get away with that this time."

He gestured wildly with his revolver toward the frightened customers.

"You three get down on the floor," he

said, "on your bellies."

"On the floor?" said the woman.

"You heard me, you old hen. If I shoot you, you'll be on the floor, won't you?"

The woman gasped and got down. The two men also lay down flat on their faces.

"Watch them, Murv," Trainor said. "Watch them close."

Murv stepped up nearer to the three prostrate customers and waved his two revolvers menacingly. His face wore a gleeful, dangerous expression.

"If any of you move," he said, "I'll kill you. You don't even have to move very much. Just a little bit. That's all."

Trainor pulled a sack loose from his belt and stepped up to the counter. He slapped the sack down in front of the bald man.

"I want to watch you fill this up," he said. "I want to see everything that goes in there. Pull the money out and show it to me."

His hands shaking, the bald man pulled out his cash drawer, and removed handfuls of bills, which he then placed on the counter in front of Trainor.

"That ain't good enough," said Trainor. "You got a safe back there?"

"Yes, but —"

"Open it."

The man started back toward the safe. Trainor went behind the counter and followed him. It took the poor little man a while to open the safe, his hands were trembling so, but finally he managed it. Trainor shoved him aside and stepped into the vault. He looked around at the stacks of bills there on the shelves.

"This is more like it," he said. "Get my sack and bring it in here."

The little man complied, and Trainor began dumping stacks of bills into the sack. At last he stopped. He hefted the bag and smiled.

"That's plenty," he said. "I don't aim to break the bank. Hell, I might want to do business here again sometime."

Then he pointed his revolver at the trembling bald man, grinned, and pulled the trigger. The banker's face registered astonished horror, and a splotch of dark red appeared in the middle of his chest. He looked for an instant as if he wanted to say something in protest, but it was too late. He fell back to lean against the wall of the vault, then slowly slid down to a sitting position. He was dead. Trainor's ears were ringing from the sound of the shot inside the vault. As soon as he had pulled the trigger, he knew he had made a mistake by firing in such close quarters.

"Damn," he said. He went back out into the lobby shaking his head and carrying the sack of money. "Let's go," he said, and the three robbers left the bank.

Outside Bobby Brown and Eli Turnbull waited with the horses. Trainor, Bardette, and Maddox mounted up, and all five men began firing their revolvers wildly. This time no one fired back. The street was empty.

"Come on," said Trainor. "Let's ride," and, his ears still ringing, he led the Border Rats out of town at a hard run, headed — once again — for the Cherokee Nation.

Ben and Dhu left the home of Middle Striker early in the morning before the sun was up. Ben was afraid that Dhu was up and around too soon, that he should have waited longer for the shoulder wound to heal up real good. But Dhu had insisted that he was perfectly fit, and so they were once again on the trail. But Ben's feelings were mixed. It might be too soon for Dhu to be traveling, but it couldn't be too soon for Katharine. Ben was afraid, on the contrary, that they might already be too late to help his sister. He was worried about her. Her letter hadn't said just how much time she had before the bank would foreclose. It might have been only a few days. She could already be out on the street with no place to live. Or she might have taken the little profit she would have from the sale and bought a ticket to Chicago or someplace. There was just no way of knowing. He was worried about his little sister Katharine.

He thought about the last time he had seen her, waving to him as he marched away to war, a skinny little kid with freckles and her hair in braids. He remembered that she had tears in her eyes as she waved goodbye standing there between their parents. Tears almost came to Ben's eyes as he recalled the moment, realizing that it was the last time he had seen, would ever see, his parents. He had, of course, considered that he would never see them again, but he had thought that it would be because he could be killed in action. It had never occurred to him that he would never see them again because they would be dead.

But Katharine alone on the farm was the problem at hand. He couldn't dwell on the past. Poor little Katharine, he thought. Alone. When he had left for the war, she had been fourteen years old. Fourteen?

"Dhu," he said, and his voice carried an urgent tone.

"What?"

"Katharine's the same age as Sam Ed."

"Is that right?" said Dhu.

"Yeah. When we first met Sam Ed, he was fourteen. Right?"

"I think so," said Dhu.

"Well, Katharine was fourteen when I left home. Same age."

"All right," said Dhu. He couldn't figure out the urgency of this information, but he didn't ask any questions.

"Well, I been thinking of Katharine just the way I last seen her. You know? I mean, how else could I think of her? But she must be all growed up by now. Sam Ed is. She must be — well, she ain't a little girl no more, is she?"

"I guess she'd be a young woman now," said Dhu. Ben shook his head slowly in wonder as they rode along.

"I never thought of that until just this minute. Katharine's all growed up. A woman. My little sister."

"Time passes the same for all of us, Ben," said Dhu.

"Yeah."

They rode on a while in silence before Ben spoke again.

"How's your shoulder?" he asked.

"It's all right," said Dhu. "Ben, quit worrying. We're going to get there okay and in time."

"I sure hope you're right," said Ben. Then he decided to try to keep quiet for a while. Dhu always thought that Ben talked too much, and Ben didn't want to give him a reason to say it again at just this time.

"Well, buddy," said Sam Ed. "You want a job here?"

"I need a job," said Bair, "but I can't believe y'all would want me."

"You a good hand?"

"Well, yeah, I think so. Good as most."

"It's settled then," said Sam Ed. "With Dhu and Ben away, we need some help around here. And I'd sure like for you to stay. We'll fix you up a place to live pretty soon so you can get out of the house here. I think we can build a pretty nice room out in the barn."

"Hell," said Charlie Bair, "I can move right on out there. I slept in barns before."

"No. You won't move until we get the room fixed up. But right now, how would you like to take a ride and look the place over?"

"Sure," said Charlie, but he was still

talking through his teeth. Sam Ed gave him a sideways look.

"You sure you're up to it?" he asked.

"It ain't my butt you busted," Charlie said. "Let's go ride."

They had looked over the corrals and the barn and were out riding the far edges of the property when the shot rang out. The two men spurred their mounts and raced into the trees.

"Where the hell did that come from?" asked Charlie.

"I ain't sure," said Sam Ed. "Whoever it is must be in the trees though, on west of us. If he was out on the prairie, we'd have seen him."

"Was he shooting at us?"

"I ain't sure," said Sam Ed. "You watch real close."

"What are you going to do?"

"I'm going to ride back out there. If he was shooting at us, he'll shoot again. You see if you can figure out where the shot's coming from."

"You might get yourself killed like that," Charlie warned.

"I hope not," said Sam Ed, and he spurred his horse. He rode hard, as if he intended to race across the prairie, and a shot sounded. The bullet kicked up dust behind his horse. He kept riding, and another shot was fired. Then he turned his mount and raced back into the trees.

"Whoa. Whoa," he said. The horse stamped and puffed. "What'd you see?" he asked.

"I think you were right," said Charlie. "It looked to me like the shot came from down there in the woods." He pointed west. The gunman was hidden, then, in the same woods as were they, just farther west.

Sam Ed thought for a moment. He looked over his shoulder, north, toward the river. "Back there's a slight rise," he said. "I think I can work my way back there and climb up on it, then move west until I come up on him. I'll be behind and above him. You stay here in case he runs out onto the prairie."

"Be careful," said Charlie.

"Don't worry," said Sam Ed. "I aim to get old. You just keep your eyes open, buddy."

Sam Ed dismounted and started walking back deeper into the woods toward the river. Soon he had climbed the rise, and he started moving west. He moved slowly, cautiously, trying to be as quiet as possible. His revolver was in his right hand, ready. Then he saw the man. He didn't have a clear view, couldn't tell who it was, but through the thicket he could see that a man was down there in the trees with a gun in his hand. He eased himself down a little closer and moved into a position where he had a clear shot. Still, he was looking at the man's back. He eased back the hammer of his revolver and leveled it at the gunman.

"You down there," he called out. "I've got you covered."

The man whirled and fired, a wild shot, and Sam Ed pulled the trigger. Birds cried out and squirrels chattered and leaves rustled overhead. Down below, the gunman slumped, fell back against a tree, then crumpled. Sam Ed moved toward him through the trees. He moved easy, stepping from one tree to another. The man didn't move. Closer, he could see the revolver on the ground beside the limp hand. He stepped on up and nudged the man. The body fell over on its side, and Sam Ed recognized the dead man just then.

He stepped out of the woods and called out to Charlie Bair.

"Charlie," he yelled. "It's okay. Come on down and bring my horse."

Charlie rode out of the woods leading Sam Ed's mount. He was with Sam Ed in a minute. He dismounted and walked into the woods again to look down on the body of the man who had shot at them from ambush.

"Hoop Roberts," he said. "I never would have thought he'd go this far."

"I sure didn't want to kill him," said Sam Ed. "Hell, all I wanted to do was to just whip him. That's all."

"Well, he didn't give you no choice," Charlie said. "If anyone wants to ask, I can tell them. I will, too."

"Yeah," said Sam Ed. "Well, we better haul him out of here. He must have left a horse somewhere around."

"I'll see if I can hunt it up," said Bair. "But where'll we take him?"

"I don't know. Back to Meriwether?"

"I guess," said Charlie. "He lived there. In the bunkhouse. We all did. I can't think of no other place."

Chapter 10

The Border Rats, being creatures of habit, stopped once again at the abandoned farmhouse that they had used before. There they counted their ill-gotten gains, and they were much more pleased than they had been the previous time. They divided the money equally, and each man stuffed his pockets full. There was money to pay for more whiskey and more women than any of them could handle at their young ages.

"Where we going to go now, Newt?" said Billy Bardette.

"Somewhere we can spend all this money, I hope," said Bobby Brown.

"You can't have a good time in these goddamned Indian Nations," said Bardette. "You got to buy a drink on the sly, and then hide out while you drink it. Let's go someplace where you can have a good time out in the open. What good's a bunch of money if you can't spend it free like you want to."

"We're wanted in Arkansas and Kansas and Missouri," said Eli Turnbull. "We got to be careful in any of them places."

113

"We ain't had so much money to spend in a long time," said Murv. His face was long. "I sure am wanting to spend some of it."

"We'll go to Texas," said Trainor. "I got it all figured out. We ain't wanted down there."

Murv's face took on a broad grin.

"Yeah," he said. "We can have a good time down there. When do we start?"

"Not right away," said Trainor. "We got some gold to get rid of first. We got to turn that into cash somehow."

"Can't we do that in Texas?" asked Bardette.

"Now where did them old boys come from?" said Trainor. "Them two cowboys we got the gold off of? Huh? Where was they from? You remember?"

"Texas," said Murv.

"And where did we figure they got the gold in the first place?" said Trainor.

"They must have stoled it," said Murv.

"So we can't take it down there and get rid of it," said Trainor. "We got to get rid of it before we go down there."

"How can we do that?" asked Eli. "I've thought and thought about that, and I can't come up with no ideas."

"You mean all them books you read don't tell you how to do that?" said

Bardette. "If them books don't give you no useful information like that, how come you waste your time reading them?"

"Reading books ain't wasting time," said Turnbull, his face turning red with anger. "It develops your brain, you dummy."

"What?" said Bardette. "Wild Willie and the Black Buffaler? Hah."

"There ain't no book named that," said Turnbull. "You don't know nothing. You —"

"Shut up," said Trainor. "I've got an idea. What we'll do is we'll ride over to old Boyd Carr's place. It wouldn't hurt none if we was to lay low for a while anyhow, and besides, I just have an idea that old Boyd might know what to do with all that gold. Course, he'll want his cut out of it, but, hell, that's all right. We get all that money, we might just not need old Boyd anymore anyhow."

Murv laughed out loud.

"No," he said. "Hell, no. We'll be rich down in Texas. We won't need old Boyd no more. That's a good one, Newt. I like that. Shit. We just won't need old Boyd no more. That dumb ass. I never liked old Boyd much anyhow, Newt."

"Come on," said Trainor. "Let's get going."

The Border Rats went outside to mount up, and Murv hesitated for a moment, looking at the remains of the Kiamichi Kid, still lying there where they had left him.

"That looks awful," he said. Scavengers had been at the body. It was obvious. "Newt, do we have to come back here again?"

"No," said Trainor. "We won't ever see this place again. We won't need to."

"Good," said Murv. "I don't want to look at that again. Or smell it. God. It's awful."

"Hell," said Billy Bardette. "That's what you're going to look like one of these days. Just like that."

"You shut your goddamned mouth," said Murv.

"Both of you shut the hell up," said Trainor. "Let's get going."

He spurred his horse and started out at a gallop, heading southeast. The others, as always, followed him.

It was late evening when the Border Rats arrived at the home of Boyd Carr, a big house with a barn and a corral just across the border of the Cherokee Nation in Arkansas. Carr was a Cherokee mixed-blood, a citizen of the Cherokee Nation, but he chose to live in Arkansas for business reasons. Some of his enterprises, such as the buying and selling of alcohol, were illegal in the Cherokee Nation, and even though some of his selling took place in the Cherokee Nation, he was safe from arrest by Cherokee authorities as long as he stayed at home. Others took the illegal beverages across the line for Carr. Others took the risks. If any questions were asked, Carr, the legitimate businessman, had conducted a simple and legal transaction in Arkansas. He had no idea what had become of the products after he had sold them.

And booze was not Carr's only business. He had purchased stolen horses and cattle on numerous occasions from Newt Trainor and others and sold them at a profit in Arkansas, Missouri, Kansas, and Texas. And he provided a safe haven for the Border Rats and others of their ilk when things got too hot for them elsewhere — for a fee, of course. No one knew what all Carr was involved in. People only knew the way in which he dealt with them, individually, and they knew that whatever he was doing, it had brought him a lot of money.

When the Border Rats rode up to the porch in front of Boyd Carr's house, the sun was low in the western sky. They had just stopped their horses, and the front door opened just enough to allow a shotgun barrel to protrude from inside.

"Who's there?" said a voice from behind the gun.

"It's Newt Trainor," said Trainor.

"And the goddamned Border Rats," yelled Murv, and he added a rebel yell and waved his hat around in a circle over his head.

The door opened wider, and Boyd Carr stepped out onto the porch, the shotgun in his right hand dangling at his side, his finger still on the trigger, thumb still on the hammer.

"Well, come on in boys," said Carr. "I ain't seen you for a while. You going to stick around a spell?"

Up on the hillside just beyond the property of Boyd Carr at a spot that afforded a clear view to the front of Carr's house, Middle Striker sat and watched as the Border Rats went into the house.

A few hours later, the Border Rats were all drunk. Eli Turnbull sat in a corner looking suspiciously out of glaring eyes, but otherwise showing no real signs of life.

Billy Bardette was spoiling for a fight, and had Newt Trainor not been there to hold him in check, he likely would have started one with the handiest person within reach of his fists. Bobby Brown was passed out on the floor, and Murv Maddox was pacing around excitedly, though excited about nothing in particular.

"You boys about ready to move on out to the bunkhouse and call it a night?" said Carr, and he yawned and stretched suggestively.

"I'm ready to talk business," said Trainor. "You know the arrangements," said Carr. "They ain't changed since last you was here."

"That ain't what I'm talking about, Boyd, old boy. I got other business. Big business."

"Won't it wait until morning?" asked Carr.

"I want to talk about it now," said Trainor.

"All right," said Carr. He picked up a bottle and poured Trainor another drink.

"What kind of big business?" he said.

"Suppose you was to lay your hands on some gold bars," said Trainor. "Pure, solid gold bars. How would you turn them gold bars into cold cash?"

"Well, now," said Carr, "I ain't exactly sure just offhand, but I reckon I'd be able to find a way. I reckon I'd be able to come up with something. Have you got yourself some of them gold bars, Newt?"

"I ain't exactly saying what I got and what I ain't got. Not just yet, I ain't. I'm just asking you a question. Could you get such a thing turned into cash?"

"Well, I damn sure wouldn't let them just lay around here taking up space. You can bet on that, boy."

"Well, suppose that they belonged to someone else," said Trainor. "How much would you charge to take on a job like that? That is, if someone was to come to you with that little problem. Just supposing."

"It ain't going to be easy," said Carr. "A job like that, I'd probably have to charge about fifty percent."

"Half and half, huh?" said Trainor.

"Fifty percent? Half?" roared Murv, who had paced up behind Carr just about then. "That ain't fair. That's too damn much."

"Shut up, Murv," said Trainor. "Me and old Boyd, we're just talking here. You just keep out of it. Go have another drink and keep your damn mouth shut. We ain't dealing here. We're just talking. Right, Boyd?"

"Uh, yeah," said Carr. "We're just supposing."

Murv went to a near corner to sulk.

"Well," said Trainor, "I suppose if a man had some of them gold bars and didn't know what to do with them, and another man knew how to get them turned into cash, I suppose that'd be worth fifty percent."

Carr leaned toward Trainor confidentially and spoke in a low voice.

"Newt," he said, "do you have some gold bars?"

"A few."

"Where are they?"

"I might show them to you when you're ready to get rid of them," said Trainor. "When could you do that?"

"If you've got them here," said Carr, "I could likely head out with them in the morning. First thing in the morning. I could be back here with the cash before dark."

"That quick? Where would you take it?"

Carr laughed and drank down his whiskey. He saw that Trainor's glass was empty, too, and he poured some more into both glasses.

"Newt," he said, "you know I ain't going to tell you that. Hell, if I was to tell you my secrets like that, you wouldn't need me no more. You give me the gold in the morning, and I'll cash it in. We'll be splitting the money before dark."

"All right," said Trainor. "In the morning."

Carr took another slug of whiskey.

"Now do you think you can get these drunks out to the bunkhouse?"

"Yeah," said Trainor. "Hell, yeah. I'll get them out of here."

He stood up, his head reeling, and surveyed the room.

"Come on, you Border Rats," he said. "Get your ass up off the floor. Come on."

They all lurched to their feet except Bobby Brown.

"Drag him along," Trainor ordered, and Murv and Bardette each grabbed one of Brown's arms. As Trainor led the way out of the house, followed by Turnbull, they dragged Brown along behind. Carr watched until they had all vanished into the big barn that contained the sleeping quarters Carr referred to as his bunkhouse. He still had a little whiskey in his glass, and he took a drink. Then he shut the door and bolted it. He didn't trust those Border Rats even when they were sober. They were the worst kind of scum, but his association with them had been profitable. And if they really did have some gold bars — how many? he wondered — if they really did have them, the association was likely to prove more profitable than ever before.

He knew just what to do. There was only one man around, to his knowledge, who had the money to buy something like that, and knew what to do with it: Nebo Drake. Carr wondered just what Drake would do with the gold once he had purchased it. He knew that Drake would get more for it than what he paid. That was just good business. The Border Rats had stolen some gold bars from somewhere. They would get some money for them. Carr would get some, a little more than he would give them, and Nebo Drake would get the most. Carr wondered if there might be some way he could find out what Drake did with the gold. He could hide and follow Drake when he took it off somewhere. But there was no guarantee that Drake would do anything with it right away, and Carr had already promised Trainor that he would return with the cash before dark.

There ought to be a way, he said to himself. Some way to spy on Drake and figure out how he does it. He sat down on the couch, fell over on his side, and was asleep almost instantly.

Out on the hillside Middle Striker still sat and watched.

Chapter 11

Katharine was in the barn securing a lead rope to her milk cow. She had arranged just that morning to sell the complacent beast to her neighbor George Phares. She expected Mr. Phares to be showing up just any time to pay her and pick up the cow, and she wanted to be ready for him. She led the cow out of the barn and tied her to the corral fence. The air was nippy. She turned to go back into the house and sucked in her breath with a start. Willard Ord was sitting there in his buggy just at the front porch of her house. He must have driven up while she was in the barn fussing with the cow. She took another breath and let it out, drew herself up to her full height, then walked toward the banker.

"Good morning, Mr. Ord," she said. "I hope you're not here to argue with me about my decision. It remains firm."

"Well, then, I won't argue, Miss Lacey," said Ord, "but it is a long drive out here, and it's a cool morning. I don't suppose I could impose on you for a cup of hot coffee before I have to head back to town?"

Katharine let out an exasperated sigh.

"You shouldn't have come all the way out here just to see me," she said, "but come in anyway," and she led the way.

Inside she put some water on the stove, and Ord walked up close behind her. When she turned around, she was almost touching him. She leaned back, away from him.

"Mr. Ord," she said. "Please have a chair."

"I want to talk to you, Katharine," he said.

"Then sit down, Mr. Ord," she said.

"Look, I don't want to hurt you. I want to be fair. Listen to me. Please."

"Mr. Ord, you're crowding me. Please move back."

Katharine tried to slip past Ord, but he grabbed her by the shoulders.

"Katharine," he said, "there is another way. Let me explain it to you. Please. Listen to me."

Katharine twisted her body, trying to break loose from Ord's grip, but he only clutched her shoulders more tightly, and he pulled her closer to him, pressing against her. His mouth searched for her mouth, but she turned her head away, still struggling to get free. She could smell the lilac water on his pudgy flesh, and she

126

could feel his hot breath. Then his wet lips opened and pressed against her neck.

"Stop it," she said. "Let me go."

"Katharine," he said, panting, "marry me. Then you'll have the farm. I'll give it to you as a wedding gift. If you still want it. If you don't want it, we'll sell it, and we'll have the money. I'll build you a fine house in town, and you'll never have to work again. You'll never have another worry, Katharine. What else can you do? I can save you, Katharine. Your worries will be over. Think about it. No more financial problems."

He stopped talking, but he was again slobbering on her neck and her ear. She flailed at him with her fists, but all she could do was pound his back. He still held her tight by the shoulders. He was still pressed against her. She reached out toward the stove with her right hand and felt for the handle of the iron skillet that she knew was there. She found it, clutched it, swung. The bottom of the skillet bounced off the side of Ord's head with a ring, and he loosened his grip and cried out in pain and shock, all at the same time.

"Ah!"

He leaned forward feeling faint, and he staggered a couple of steps, but he managed to stay on his feet. His left hand went up to the side of his head, and he could feel the sticky blood beginning to trickle down his temple toward his cheek. He backed away from Katharine, still leaning forward, holding his head. With his right hand, he pulled a handkerchief out of his pocket, and he began to daub with it at the blood on his head.

"Ah," he groaned. "Oh."

"Get out of my house this instant, Mr. Ord," said Katharine. "Just who do you think you are? What do you think I am? You ought to be ashamed of yourself."

Ord looked up at Katharine, an expression of horror on his face. He stood for a frantic moment, then he turned and rushed out of the house. As he clambered up into the seat of his buggy, George Phares came driving up in his wagon. Ord shot Phares a quick, desperate glance and grabbed up the reins of his buggy. He snapped the reins viciously.

"Mr. Ord?" said Phares. "What's the matter?"

Ord lashed at his horse and raced off without a word. Phares stared after him as Katharine stepped out onto the porch.

"Miss Lacey," said Phares, "is anything wrong here?"

"No, Mr. Phares," said Katharine. "Everything's fine. Thank you. I have the cow waiting for you over here."

Phares looked at Katharine for a moment, questioning, but she said nothing more. He climbed down from his wagon and walked over to inspect the cow. He had seen her before and well knew what he was buying. It was just a matter of form. Then he dug into his pockets for his money and paid Katharine. He took the cow over to the wagon and tied her to the back.

"Miss Lacey," he said, "are you sure everything's all right here?"

"Yes, Mr. Phares. I'm quite sure. Thank you."

Phares drove away with his cow, and Katharine went back into the house. She put away the money. She had work to do, and she tried to put Ord out of her mind, but she couldn't. Whatever could have gotten into him? she wondered. What did he think of her? The more she thought about it, the angrier she got, and she found herself breathing hard and trembling.

"Damn him," she said out loud, and that, too, surprised her, and she was even angrier with the banker for causing her to react in that way. She prided herself on her patience and calm, and Ord had shaken that calm. She didn't like losing control that way. Well, she would just have to get hold of herself. There was work to be done.

Of course, she realized, her situation was even more hopeless now than before. If there had ever been a chance that Ord would relent, it was gone now. For good. He would foreclose now with glee, with a vengeance.

There was no telling what the man might do next. Would he simply sit in his bank and wait for the date to come around? Or would he come back? She remembered her papa's gun, and she went to get it out of the closet in the bedroom that had been her parents'. She didn't know much about guns. It was a rifle of some kind. And she remembered that Papa had always kept it loaded. She found the rifle and took it out of the closet. She examined it closely. It had a hammer on the side. She knew enough to know that she would have to pull back that hammer before she could fire the weapon. She carried it into the living room and propped it in a corner near the front door. If Willard Ord should dare come back after what he had done, she would be ready for him.

Then she had a sudden image in her mind of Willard Ord coming toward her out in front of her house. In her mind, she was standing on the porch, and she was holding the rifle. She saw herself thumb back the hammer and lift the heavy weapon to her shoulder. Ord came closer. His face was red and puffy, and it wore a menacing leer. He was sweating, and he was panting, and he was coming closer, and then she pulled the trigger, and there was a deafening roar and a cloud of smelly blue smoke rose up around her. She blinked her eyes and fought to clear her head of the unpleasant image. She didn't want to see the next part. She didn't want to see Ord as the bullet crashed into his flabby guts and the blood splattered. She didn't want to watch him fall, and she didn't want to look at the lifeless form lying there on the ground in front of her house.

She took a deep breath and went to the stove where the water she had put on earlier was boiling violently. She moved the pot off the fire and went outside to breathe the cool air, to clear her head.

Willard Ord raced his buggy at full speed for about a mile before he was able to think halfway clearly and slow it down. Damn it, he thought, I could kill the horse like this. He brought the buggy to a stop, leaned back against the seat, and breathed deeply for a moment. His head felt hot and light. His heart was pounding.

"God," he said, "what have I done? What came over me back there? Oh God. Oh God."

He knew that he would be ruined if Katharine told anyone in town what had happened. His reputation would be ruined. He could lose his bank, perhaps even his freedom. He could lose everything. He wouldn't be able to stand that, he knew. And what about his mother? What would she say if she heard about it? He hated to think about that possibility. But what could he do? It was done. He had actually attacked the girl. He had done it before he realized what he was doing. What had he thought? That she would accept him? That she would want him as badly as he wanted her? That she was so alone and so desperate that she would accept any proposal, no matter how distasteful? Sitting alone in his buggy well after the fact, he realized that such a thought was ridiculous. How could she find anything attractive in him? Anything except his money. He was middle-aged and overweight, and his face was not handsome. He had never been much to look at, even in his youth. He had nothing to offer, nothing but his money.

And now would he lose his money? What did they do with a man's money when they sent him to prison? He couldn't bear the thought of being broke and of being disgraced. He couldn't bear the thought of prison. He would have to think of something. He had to do something. Frantic thoughts raced through his mind, thoughts of murder and of suicide. He thought of packing a bag with clothes and cash and fleeing the country, but where would he go with his money? He didn't know. California? New York? Somewhere overseas perhaps? He had to think of something. He had to do something. He couldn't allow that girl to ruin his life, no matter what he had done.

Ben felt closer to home all at once when they finally rode into Missouri. And, of course, he told himself, he was closer to home. He knew that it was a long way yet across Missouri, but Missouri was just next door to Iowa. It was not far from his old home in southern Iowa to the Missouri border, so he was feeling close to home in

Missouri. He even began to feel a little cocky, more sure of himself somehow. Ever since he had known Dhu Walker, he had been in unfamiliar territory. Now the tables were about to turn. Ben was close to home, and soon Dhu Walker would be the stranger in a strange land. Ben liked that feeling.

"We ain't safe yet, Dhu," he said. "Missouri's pretty rough country. We've got a lot of outlaws up here. Bad ones. It's always been that way."

"Not always," said Dhu. "Just ever since the white man showed up."

Ben felt his ears burn. Dhu always got the best of him somehow.

"You mean there wasn't no bad Indians?" Ben said.

"Back before there were any white folks here?" said Dhu. "Oh, I'm sure there were some bad Indians. There's good and bad among all kinds of people. But I don't believe that we had any outlaws among us in those days. A few troublemakers, I guess. Bullies maybe. And we had ways of dealing with them. But no outlaws. We didn't need them. If we got out too far away from home, we had other tribes to deal with."

Ben wasn't sure just what Dhu meant by all that, and he was afraid that maybe Dhu had been right when he said that Ben just wasn't equipped for thinking.

"Well," he said, "does that mean that things was better back then?"

"No better and no worse," said Dhu. "Just different."

They rode on for a while without saying anything, and then Dhu spoke again.

"It was probably a whole lot better for the Indians," he said.

Chapter 12

Nebo Drake lived in a place about as secluded and protected as could be had. In order to get to Drake's establishment, one had to ride through a narrow pass with high boulders on either side. At least one armed guard or lookout could usually be seen atop the boulders — one of Drake's many brothers or cousins. Sometimes the guard would wave the visitor on through the pass. Other times he would challenge the visitor, demanding his name and the nature of his business. Even a large and well-armed force would have found it difficult to assault Nebo Drake's stronghold. Visitors, or customers, never knew how many armed men were in and around the place. They seldom came into close contact with anyone other than Drake, but they often saw armed men at a distance, half-hidden, watching.

When Boyd Carr rode up to the pass, he looked up. He felt a bit nervous. It was natural to feel so, he told himself, with an armed man high overhead. The man above lifted a rifle high over his head and waved it, a sign for Carr to ride on in. Carr removed his hat and waved it back in acknowledgment, then urged his horse forward. In another few moments he was tying the horse to the hitch rail in front of Drake's house or place of business. It might have been both. Carr suspected that it was.

It was a small house made mostly of logs. Actually it appeared to be two small houses constructed back to back so as to serve as a two-room house. The logs were uneven, and the roof had a distinct sag in the middle. The windows were hung from the inside with dirty canvas. A wolf skin was tacked carelessly to the front door. An old hound was sleeping on the porch just to the right of the doorway. Flies swarmed over its unconcerned figure. Carr thought at first that the dog was dead, but then he saw its chest heave once.

He looked up from the rail as he heard the sound of the door opening, followed by footsteps on the porch. Nebo Drake stood there with his hands in his pockets and a wad of chewing tobacco in his left cheek. He spat on the dog's rump, but the dog made no reaction whatsoever.

"Hello, Boyd," said Drake. "It's been a while."

"Yes," said Carr. "It has been."

"Come on inside and have a drink with me," said Drake. "I know you've had a long ride."

"I'll have one," said Carr, "but that's all. I have the same long ride back still ahead of me. I have to be back before dark."

He followed Drake inside. As always, it was dark in the interior of Drake's establishment. The house had few windows, and they were small and shuttered and curtained by the ragged pieces of dirty canvas. Carr wondered why they were even there. He couldn't recall ever having seen them open. And the air was dank and damp and seemed to Carr to be unhealthy.

Drake poured two drinks of whiskey, and Carr happily accepted one of them. He sipped at it, trying to ignore the dust on the glass. Drake gulped his own down and poured himself another.

"What brings you over?" he asked.

"I've got some goods I need to unload," said Carr.

Drake tossed down the rest of his second drink.

"Let's have a look," he said, turning his head to one side in order to spit across the room.

Carr stood up. He finished his drink and set the glass down on the table.

"It's out on the horse," he said.

"Bring it in," said Drake. He poured whiskey in both glasses while Carr went back outside. In a couple of minutes, Carr returned, carrying, with some difficulty, a set of saddlebags. He struggled over to the table and tossed them on it. Dust scattered in all directions.

"Heavy," said Drake.

Carr, puffing from the exertion, unbuckled the straps that held the flap down on the bags, opened the flaps, and pulled out a bar of gold. Drake looked at the bar. He showed no excitement, no real reaction. Carr thought about the hound out on the porch.

"You got more in there?" asked Drake.

Carr pulled out the rest. Drake sat in silence for a long moment, studying the gold bars and rubbing his chin. He leaned forward to spit on the floor between his feet. Then he opened a drawer in the table and removed a smudged and rumpled piece of paper and a stub of a pencil. He wrote a figure down and shoved the paper toward Carr. It scooped up dust from the tabletop like a shovel.

"That's what gold is worth just now," said Drake, and he watched Carr's eyes light up. Then he pulled the paper back and wrote another figure. He shoved the paper at Carr again. "That's all I can give you for it."

Boyd Carr studied the figures on the piece of paper. He had to do some quick calculating in his head to see what kind of an offer Drake was making. It was about fifty percent of the value of the merchandise. It was really all he expected. After all, the stuff was stolen, and Drake wouldn't be able to dispose of it at full value. And Drake had to make his profit. Carr wished again that he knew Drake's secrets. He put the paper back on the table.

"You have the cash on hand?" he asked.

"Of course," said Drake. "If I didn't have it, I wouldn't have made the offer."

"All right," said Carr, extending his hand, "I'll take it."

Drake took the hand and grinned, showing brown-stained teeth.

"I figured you would," he said. He poured two more glasses of whiskey and drank his down by the time Carr got his up to his lips to sip.

"Wait here," Drake said. He ducked through a doorway that was hung with an old, soiled sheet. In a few moments he returned with a stack of bills. He counted them out on the table. "There you are," he said. "It's always good doing business with you, Boyd. Be careful going home with all that money. There's outlaws out there, you know."

Drake stood on his porch and watched as Boyd Carr rode away. Boyd Carr was in for some trouble, he thought. He'd eat his hat if that gold wasn't from the same batch Dhu Walker had been bringing him over the last three or four years. Drake knew that Carr hadn't gotten it from Walker. He also knew that Carr did business with the Border Rats. It was logical then to assume that the Border Rats had stolen Walker's gold. Well, Drake thought, if they didn't kill him while they were at it, they'd be sorry. Dhu Walker wasn't likely to forget.

The mortgage payment was due at last, and Katharine did not have the money. She didn't know exactly what the procedure would be. She thought that Willard Ord might come out to the farm with the sheriff and some official papers of some kind to make her leave the farm. Or perhaps she should go in to the bank and surrender it voluntarily. She just didn't know. Nothing like this had ever happened to her before.

And what about all her belongings? She

realized that she had been a fool. She had sold everything she could in an attempt to raise the money, but she was far short of the amount she needed. And now she had no horses to pull the wagon. She had no transportation other than her saddle horse. She would have to abandon her things along with the farm. She was sure that Ord would show no mercy.

She finished her breakfast and went outside. Looking around, she thought about all the chores that needed to be done.

"But it's not my farm anymore," she said out loud. "Oh, what the hell."

She saddled her horse and rode toward town.

Ord saw her coming. He hurried into his office and shuffled some papers around on his desk. Then he tried to appear to be busy with something. In a few minutes, Katharine was in his office. He looked up at her, and his face turned red.

"Uh, good morning, Miss Lacey," he said. "Please sit down."

Katharine sat in a chair facing Ord. The banker resumed his seat. Nervously, he fussed with the papers on his desk.

"I'll get right to it, Mr. Ord," said Katharine. "I don't have the money. I came in to tell you that I've left the farm. It's yours."

"Miss Lacey," said Ord, "I deeply regret the events of our last meeting."

"Yes," said Katharine. "I'm sure you do. And so do I."

"My behavior was inexcusable."

"To say the least."

"I've been — I've been afraid ever since that day."

"Afraid, Mr. Ord? What in the world have you been afraid of?"

Ord stood up and paced away from his desk. He stood facing the wall, his back to Katharine.

"Well," he said, "under the circumstances, that is, after what happened out there, uh, what I did, or rather —"

"Oh," said Katharine, "I see. You've been afraid that I might have said something to someone. Is that it?"

"Well, yes."

"You can rest assured, Mr. Ord, that I have not mentioned that incident to anyone, nor do I intend to. I see no reason to pursue it. I have no desire to take advantage of you for any reason. Now, if we can get on with our business, please. Is there something I have to sign, or do I simply walk away?"

Ord went back to his desk and sat down. He picked up a paper and handed it across the desk to Katharine. She took it and looked at it.

"What is this?" she said.

"It's a transfer of the property from you to me," said Ord. "It's a bill of sale."

Katharine gave Ord a puzzled look.

"I don't understand," she said.

"Well," said Ord, his face growing even redder, "it's really quite simple. I haven't been fair with you. And now you've been more than fair with me. I'm . . . I'm more than a little ashamed of myself. This is, I think, a fair offer for your farm. A fair price."

"It's more than a fair price," said Katharine. "I think it's about two thousand dollars too much. Are you making me a new offer?"

"Yes. For that amount. It will pay off the mortgage and leave you with —"

"A substantial sum. I see that. If you'll lower the offer by two thousand dollars, I'll accept it."

"Well, of course. I will. If that's what you want."

"It is."

"Miss Lacey, there is one other thing."

Katharine looked at Ord with suspicion. She had been expecting a catch somewhere along the line.

"Yes?" she said.

"If you really don't want to sell, I'm willing to grant you an extension, to give you more time to pay off the mortgage. It's up to you."

"Mr. Ord, I don't know what's come over you. But I've learned something in the time we've been fighting with each other. I've learned that I can't handle the farm alone. I'll take your purchase offer at the figure I mentioned."

"Yes. Well, if you'll just sign the paper, I'll mark the mortgage paid and give you your money."

"All of my things are still out there, Mr. Ord. Will you allow me time to collect them and move them out?"

"Of course. All the time you need."

Standing outside the bank, Katharine took in deep breaths of fresh air. Her purse contained the bank note marked paid and more cash than she ever thought she would have at one time. She could hardly believe her good fortune. She had come into town fully expecting to lose everything, and instead she had experienced a complete reversal of fortune. Who would ever have thought, she said to herself, that Willard Ord's despicable behavior would turn out to be my salvation? Who would ever have thought it?

The sun was almost down when Boyd Carr arrived back at his home in Arkansas. He could see that the lamps were lit in his house, and he burned with irritation. The Border Rats had no business being in his house while he was away. There was nothing wrong with the quarters in the barn. They had everything they needed in there.

"Damn it," he said.

He took his horse to the barn, and he took his time. Let them wait, he said to himself. He was strolling back toward the house with his saddlebags thrown over his shoulder, and he saw Newt Trainor step out onto his front porch.

"Welcome back," said Trainor. "I was beginning to think you'd run out on us. I was thinking about going after you."

"Bullshit," said Carr. "This is my home. Would I leave it to you? It's a long ride over there and back."

"Over where, Boyd?" asked Trainor, a sly look on his face.

"Never you mind where," said Carr. "But it's a long damn ride."

He pushed past Trainor and went inside. Trainor followed. Carr tossed the saddlebags on a table, opened them up, and poured out the contents.

"God damn," said Trainor, his eyes wide with astonishment. "That's more money than I ever seen before."

"I've already taken out my fifty percent," said Carr. "That's all yours. Where are your boys?"

"Ah," said Trainor, "they're all passed out in the other room."

"I wish you had stayed out in the bunkhouse," said Carr. "I'd rather not have them passed out here in my house."

Trainor was fondling the stacks of bills on the table.

"They ain't hurting nothing," he said. "Hell, they ain't even moving. I told you. They're passed out. They might as well be dead. How could they hurt anything?"

Carr sipped from his drink.

"I guess you boys will be moving on now," said Carr. "Texas?"

"There ain't no hurry, is there?" said Trainor. "Won't nobody look for us here, will they? Why, I imagine we could stay here for six months and be just as safe as anything."

Carr gritted his teeth, but he knew that he had to keep calm.

"I don't know," he said. "The law has

been acting suspicious of me lately. I wouldn't be too sure of being safe here. I'd be careful if I had the law after me just now."

"Oh, yeah? Well, maybe you're right. Maybe we ought to go. Go to Texas. Texas is a big place. The laws could look for a fellow for a long time in Texas and never even cross his tracks. Ain't that right?"

"Yeah," said Carr. "It's a big place all right. Look, I've had a long day. I'm tired, and I want to turn in. Can you get those guys out of here? Take them all back out to the bunkhouse."

Trainor eased his revolver out of its holster and pointed it carelessly at Carr's chest. Carr's jaw dropped.

"What —"

"Boyd," said Trainor, "I'm just about sick of you. You're plenty glad to get my business. My money's plenty good for you. But you don't like me and my boys in your house. You don't even want us around once you've got your hands on some of my money. You think you're too good for us or something. Well, right now I've got more money than I'll ever know what to do with, and I don't think I'll be needing you anymore."

"Wait a minute, Newt," said Carr, his voice trembling. "There's not all that much money. You'll spend all that before you know it, and you'll be needing more. Hey. Money ain't what it used to be. It goes real fast these days."

"I'll have more when I take your share," said Trainor, and he pulled the trigger. Carr didn't have time to scream. He opened his mouth just as the bullet struck him. He looked down at the bloody hole in his chest, and his body began to go limp. His eyes took on a glazed appearance, and he slumped to the floor — dead.

Trainor holstered his revolver and looked down at Carr's body to watch the widening pool of dark blood spread from underneath.

"You still too good, Boyd?" he said. "Huh? You ain't too good for nothing now. By God, that might have taught you a lesson in good manners if it hadn't killed you."

He picked up the glass Carr had been drinking from and drank it dry. Then he refilled it from Carr's bottle. He took another taste and smacked his lips.

"By damn," he said, "you even kept the best whiskey back for just your own self, didn't you? You cheap skunk. You wanted me and my boys out of your old house? Your old smelly house? Well, I'll be getting out pretty soon. Pretty damn soon."

Chapter 13

Dhu had never seen so many cornfields in his whole life, and he was beginning to hope that he would never see another. There seemed to be no end to them, and the corn was so tall that a man could get lost in it and never find his way out again. And the land was flat. He had never seen such flat land. It was enough to make a man — what? He decided that perhaps he had just discovered what was really wrong with Ben Lacey. The poor wretch had grown up and spent almost all his life in this flat country covered with endless cornfields. It seemed to explain a lot somehow.

Then they came to a corner. The cornfield ended there, and there was an empty space. It wasn't really empty. It was like a big yard, and on its other side were more cornfields. A narrow lane cut through the yard at right angles from the road, and at the far end of the lane was a small frame house. In front of the house a wagon was parked. Ben stopped his horse, so Dhu pulled up beside him.

"Well," said Ben, leaning wearily on his

saddle horn, "there it is. That there is the place where I grew up at."

He could scarcely believe that they had finally made it. It seemed to Ben like the longest journey he had ever made, and here he was, once again looking at the old home place. He had wondered for the last four years if he would ever see it again. The long trip across Missouri had been totally uneventful, tedious, boring even. Ben had been a little disappointed in that. After all, he had warned Dhu about the bad Missouri outlaws, and he had been hoping to be of more use, maybe even to have been consulted a time or two there in his own home territory, but nothing had occurred to merit that. Things had been the same as always. Dhu had been in charge. Dhu had selected the campsites and determined the time to stop at the end of the day and the time to start in the mornings.

Of course, Ben had not really wanted to be attacked by outlaws, but he had hoped for something different. Oh well, he thought, the trip was over, and Katharine would be waiting just there at the farm. At least he hoped that she would be.

"That's the place, you say?" said Dhu.

"Yeah. That's it."

"So what are we waiting for?"

"Nothing, I guess," said Ben. "Come on."

They rode forward, and as they drew closer, they could see that the wagon parked in front of the house was loaded with trunks and suitcases. The two riders hesitated and looked at each other.

"Damn it," said Ben. "We're too late."

"Maybe not," said Dhu. "At least she's still here if she's still packing. Come on. Let's find out what's going on."

They raced on to the farmhouse, and Ben dismounted quickly. He ran for the porch while Dhu secured the horses.

"Katharine?" Ben shouted. "Sis! Are you in there?"

Katharine stepped out onto the porch, astonishment on her face.

"Ben?" she said. Then she saw him. "Ben! I can't believe it! Oh, I — I had no idea you were on the way up here."

She threw her arms around his neck and hugged him tight. Then she stepped back to look him in the face, and tears came into her eyes.

"Ain't you glad to see me?" said Ben.

"Oh, Ben," she said.

"I'm sorry I wasn't here," said Ben. "I should have been. I guess it's really been rough on you. Here all by yourself. I should have come home after the war. I knew I should have, but I was just thinking of only myself. I'm sorry, Sis."

"No. Don't be. You have a right to your own life. Your own family. I'm just sorry that Mama and Papa weren't able to see you at least once more," she said. "Other than that, I guess it hasn't been too bad. It could have been a lot worse, I guess."

She glanced at Dhu, standing quietly beside the porch, and there was a moment of awkward silence.

"Oh," said Ben. "This here is Dhu, my partner. Dhu Walker, that is. Dhu, this is my sister, Katharine."

Dhu took off his hat and held it in both hands. He tried not to stare. This was a beautiful young woman, hardly what he had expected. Then he asked himself just what he had expected to find. Just how had he pictured Ben's sister? He wasn't really aware of having pictured her at all, yet if he hadn't, why was he so surprised? So pleasantly surprised?

"How do you do?" he said.

"I'm fine, thank you, Mr. Walker," said Katharine. "I'm just a little embarrassed and ashamed of myself though. And I'm such a mess. I wasn't expecting company."

"Oh, you look just fine, ma'am," said Dhu, and he meant it, every word.

She turned again toward Ben. "I guess my second letter didn't reach you in time," she said.

"No," said Ben. "I only got just the one. What is it? Has something else happened?"

"Oh no," said Katharine, "nothing like that. I really don't know what to say. I shouldn't have written what I did. I know that you're both too busy to come running up here just because of what I wrote. And it's such a long way. I wrote you again to tell you that everything was all right. I'm sorry."

"But you're loading a wagon, Miss Lacey," said Dhu.

"Yes. I'm moving out."

"Then you lost the farm?" said Ben.

"No. I sold it, and at a good price. Half the money is yours, of course, Ben. I meant to send it to you, but now that you're here I won't have to do that."

"Don't be silly, Katharine," said Ben. "It's all yours. I don't need the money. I want you to keep it."

"So where are you going?" asked Dhu.

"Well, I — I'm not sure. But I'll be all right. I'll figure something out."

"You mean," said Dhu, "you don't have any specific plans?"

"Well, no. I don't just yet," she said.

"But I have money. All I have to do is make up my mind where I want to live. It's really kind of nice. I've never had that kind of freedom before."

"I know," said Ben. "You're coming with us — back to Texas."

"Oh, I don't know," said Katharine. "I wouldn't want to be in the way. What would I do in Texas?"

"You wouldn't be in the way," said Ben. "We've got plenty of room. Ain't we, Dhu?"

"Sure we have," said Dhu. "You're welcome at the LWM any time, and for as long as you want to stay. Why, you're a whole lot prettier than your brother, and we've allowed him to hang around for four years."

Katharine turned away just a little from the two men and stared off over the vast, swaying cornfields.

"I would like to meet my sister-in-law," she said, "and my new niece. And I really don't have any other plans."

"Then it's settled," said Ben. "Have you got more stuff to load up?"

"A little."

"Then let's get it done and get you out of here."

Katharine had been thinking that she

was alone with no place to go, and she had packed only her clothes and a few small things that she couldn't bear to part with. She had thought that she would abandon her furniture and the other household goods. But with Ben and Dhu to help her, and with a place to go, she decided to take it all. Well, most of it. At least, a lot more than she had thought at first. They nearly emptied the house and loaded the wagon full. The wagon was stacked high, and the load securely tied. Then they were ready to go, but the day was about to come to an end.

"What do we do now?" said Katharine. "It's too late to start traveling, isn't it?"

"We should wait until morning," said Dhu. "We wouldn't get very far tonight anyhow, especially with this wagon."

"But everything's packed. I can't fix us any supper. And where will we sleep?"

"Let's go into town," said Ben. "We can eat at the café and spend the night in the hotel."

The meal was good. Katharine hadn't eaten out in a long time. Her father had been too frugal for such things, and since his death, she hadn't had either the time or the money to spare. For Ben and Dhu, it was a relief to eat something besides camp cooking. Ben saw several old friends and talked with them, each catching up with the other. At one point in the evening, Ben left the table to speak with an old acquaintance, and Dhu and Katharine sat alone. They sat there for a moment, silent, hesitant.

"It was awfully good of you to accompany Ben on this trip, Mr. Walker," said Katharine.

"It wasn't any bother," said Dhu. "I had business in the Cherokee Nation anyhow, and it's good to get away from the ranch now and then. But, please, Miss Lacey, call me Dhu."

"I will," she said, "if you'll call me Katharine."

"All right, Katharine."

"You have an unusual name," she said.

"Dhu? Yes. I'm always getting questions about it. My full name is Roderick Dhu Walker. It's from —"

"*The Lady of the Lake*," said Katharine. "Of course. I should have known."

"You know the poem?" said Dhu.

" 'These are Clan-Alpine's warriors true,' " quoted Katharine, " 'and, Saxon, I am Roderick Dhu.' "

"You do know it," he said with a pleasant chuckle.

"It's one of my favorites. You seem surprised. We have books and schools in Iowa."

"Sure," said Dhu. "I guess it's just that, well, you're Ben's sister, and Ben —"

"Ben never did very well in school," said Katharine. "Papa used to have to take a stick to him to get him to read anything. It was almost as if it hurt Ben to read. He always wanted to be outside doing something, getting dirty."

"I should learn to stop making assumptions about people," said Dhu.

"You seem to be well educated," said Katharine. "When Ben wrote to me, he said that you're an Indian. Are you?"

"Yes. I'm a Cherokee," said Dhu. "Well, I'm half white, but I was born and raised a Cherokee, and I'm a citizen of the Cherokee Nation."

"You're not a United States citizen?"

"No."

"Where did you get your education?"

"In the Cherokee Nation. We have our own school system, including male and female seminaries. I even taught school for a while."

"Why did you quit?"

"I don't know. It's funny. The only thing I can think of is what you said about Ben a while ago. You said that he always wanted to be outside doing something, rather than be in school. It never occurred to me until just this moment that I might have that in common with him. I quit to go home and work with my father raising horses. Then the war came along. My parents were killed. The horses were stolen. I was caught up in the war. I got captured, and then I escaped with Ben. We wound up down in Texas with the McClellans and built up the LWM Ranch. Raising and training and selling fine horses. Now you know my life story."

Katharine laughed, a pleasant laugh, Dhu thought.

"I'm sure there's more to it than that," she said. "And, you know, you're not the only one guilty of making assumptions about other people."

"Oh?"

"I would never have thought to meet an educated Indian, especially one educated in his own tribal schools. Is that the proper term?"

"Yes," said Dhu. "It will do."

"When Ben wrote to me about you, I pictured somebody, well, wild."

"I can be pretty wild sometimes. Ask your brother."

Katharine laughed again, and Dhu liked it even better than the first time.

"What about you?" he said.

"What?"

"Tell me your life story."

"You've already seen it," said Katharine. "The farm. That's been my whole life. There's nothing else to tell."

"Have you ever traveled?"

"No. Just to this town."

"This trip to Texas is going to be a major change in your life then," said Dhu.

"Yes, it is. And I'm a little afraid."

"Are you?"

"Not much. Not anymore. I have a feeling that you could take care of just about anything that came up."

"Well, I, uh, I don't know about that," said Dhu. "I'll do my best. Katharine?"

"Yes?"

"I hope you won't think I'm trying to be forward, but Ben said we were coming up here to rescue his poor little sister. She was just a kid, he said. Well, he couldn't have been more wrong."

"Oh?"

"You're a beautiful woman," said Dhu, and having said it, he was aware that he had embarrassed both himself and Katharine. "Well," he said, "I think it's about time we all turned in — if we want to get an early start."

Katharine's face was slightly flushed.

"Yes," she said. "I think you're right."

Dhu dreamed that night of Katharine Lacey. He relived the conversation over the dinner table with her, and he took her for a long walk across the rolling prairie of north Texas. He saddled a beautiful white horse for her, and then they rode together for miles, and he watched her hair blowing back in the wind. He heard her musical laugh, and once he reached out to touch her cheek, and it was smooth and soft and just a little cool. And he was going to kiss her lips. He felt daring and bold, and he moved closer to her, and then he woke up and saw that it was morning. Soon it would be time to get started. He crawled out of bed with a groan and started to get dressed.

Chapter 14

Sam Ed McClellan and Charlie Bair took the wagon into Preston. They went to pick up the mail and to get a few supplies. It did not take two men to accomplish those two simple chores, but Herd insisted that Charlie accompany Sam Ed. He didn't want Sam Ed to be caught out alone just in case there was any trouble. They had taken care of their chores, the wagon was loaded and ready to go.

"How about a beer before we head back?" said Charlie.

Sam Ed hesitated a moment in thought. Herd would not approve, and certainly Maude wouldn't. But Sam Ed in his own mind was a grown man. He could make his own decisions. And he did like a cold beer now and then.

"Why not?" he said.

The two young men walked across the street together and went into Gerald McDaniel's saloon. The place was not crowded. There were plenty of empty tables, and no one was standing at the bar. Sam Ed and Charlie opted for the bar.

McDaniel stepped over to serve them.

"I still can't get used to seeing you two boys together," he said. "Wonders never ceases, do they? What'll you have?"

"Two beers," said Charlie. "Ain't no wonder about it, Gerald. Old Sam Ed here whipped me so bad, I can't afford to have him for an enemy no more. I got to be his friend, hell."

"Ah, shut up, Charlie," said Sam Ed.

McDaniel got the beers and put them on the counter. Sam Ed paid for them.

"I don't suppose you boys have seen Thane Savage in town today?" said McDaniel.

"Nope," said Sam Ed. "Not today."

"Ain't seen him," said Charlie. "Ain't looking for him either."

"I don't particularly care if I never see him again, come to think of it," said Sam Ed.

"Well, I didn't think you'd seen him," said McDaniel. "He was in here last night. He said some pretty tough things about the both of you. Said he'd kill you both on sight."

Sam Ed and Charlie gave each other a look.

"He can try," said Sam Ed. "I ain't looking to kill him. Just to whip him. But if he tries to kill me, I'll for sure protect myself. Whatever way I have to."

"I ain't interested in him at all," said Charlie. "I used to work with Thane, and I ain't got nothing against him. But just like Sam Ed said, if he tries anything with me, I'll damn sure protect myself."

McDaniel shrugged.

"Well," he said, "it's got nothing to do with me one way or the other. I'm just passing on what I heard him say. Thought you might be interested."

"We are," said Sam Ed. "Sure. Thanks, Gerald."

They finished their beers and wiped their mouths on their shirtsleeves.

"Well, we better be getting back," said Sam Ed.

"See you, Gerald," said Charlie, and he turned and headed for the door. Sam Ed was just a few steps behind him.

"Oh, Sam Ed," said McDaniel. "I got that bottle of Kentucky sipping whiskey your daddy ordered. You want to pick it up for him?"

"Sure."

Sam Ed went back to the bar digging in his pocket for some money. Charlie walked on outside. On the boardwalk he looked up to see Thane Savage blocking his path.

"Charlie Bair," said Savage. "This here

must be my lucky day. I been looking for you, you traitor bastard."

"Hello, Thane," said Charlie. "Funny. We was just talking about you. Somebody said you been bragging you was going to kill me."

"I mean to," said Savage. "Go for your gun."

"I got no quarrel with you, Thane."

"Well, I got one with you."

"I don't want to fight you," said Charlie. "We was friends."

"Was is right, and I can't figure out why I didn't see through you right away," said Savage. "Or at least why I didn't see that yellow stripe down your back."

"I was hurt, Thane, and I tried to get word to Mr. Meriwether, but by the time I got it to him, he'd done replaced me. The McClellans offered me a job, and I took it. Anything wrong with that?"

"I never thought I'd see a friend of mine team up with blue-bellied Yankees," said Savage.

"The war's over," said Charlie, "and the McClellans are good folks. Ranching's ranching, and a job's a job. Let it go."

"I ain't letting go," said Savage. "Go for your gun, or I'll kill you anyway, right where you stand."

"I ain't going to do it, Thane."

"Then I'll kill you anyways."

"You'll drop next," said Sam Ed. He had just stepped out the door. He held the whiskey bottle in his left hand. His right was ready to draw his revolver. Thane Savage looked from one man to the other.

"I ain't going to take on both of you at once," he said.

"Take one," said Sam Ed. "Take me. Fists or guns. Either way you want it. I'm ready now. Come on."

"There'll be another time," said Savage.

He turned and walked away, and Sam Ed and Charlie watched him go. Then they went back to their wagon and headed for the LWM.

"There's going to be a showdown with him yet," said Charlie as they rode out of town.

"You damn bet you there is," said Sam Ed. "If he don't press it, I will."

Dhu Walker picked a spot beside a clear, flowing stream to camp for the night. He and Ben and Katharine had been on the trail for a good long stretch. It wasn't their first camp. It wouldn't be the last. Katharine was holding up well, surprising both Ben and Dhu. The camp set up, they cooked themselves a meal and ate. A little later, with cups of hot coffee, they were seated around the fire making small talk. The night was clear, and the stars were bright.

"We'll be back in the Cherokee Nation tomorrow," said Dhu.

"I never dreamed of traveling so far," said Katharine.

"You ain't sorry you came along, are you, Sis?" said Ben.

"Oh, no. I'm glad to be here. With you. With you both. But I'll be even happier to have the trip over and done."

"I think we all will be," said Dhu. "It's a long haul."

"I'm really anxious to meet your family, Ben, and the rest of the McClellans," said Katharine. "They sound like awfully nice people. And my own niece. I haven't figured out yet what it feels like to be an aunt. How much longer do you think it will be?"

Ben looked at Dhu. Neither of them had said anything to Katharine about the Border Rats and their plans to pursue them. Ben was feeling a little guilty at having concealed that information from his sister for so long.

"Well," he said, "that all depends. Dhu, when we get in the Cherokee Nation — what then?"

Dhu gave Ben a sharp look.

"We ride on through," he said. "What else?"

"What about — you know? What we talked about before?"

"We'll talk about it later," said Dhu. "There's plenty of time for that."

"What?" said Katharine. "What is it you're talking about?"

"Oh, nothing," said Ben. "Just some business we had in the Cherokee Nation. We talked about taking care of it on the way through, but, like Dhu says, it'll wait."

"You mean you'll take me to Texas and then come back for your business?" said Katharine.

"Yeah," said Ben. He felt foolish for having caused this conversation to take place, and he knew that he had made Dhu mad at him again because of his big mouth. "I guess so."

"We won't have to turn right around and come back," said Dhu. "It's not all that urgent."

"I remember now," said Katharine, looking at Dhu, "that you told me you had come along with Ben on this trip because of business you had along the way. I don't want to be the cause of any inconvenience to you. If you have business, take care of it.

Don't pamper me. Please."

Dhu heaved a heavy sigh, and then scowled at Ben.

"All right," he said, "I'll tell you. On our way up north, we were robbed. We were afraid that your situation was urgent, so we just rode on. And we planned to track down those bandits on the way back. But we didn't know that we'd have you with us, and I don't think that we should put you in any danger."

"I see," said Katharine. "So I have spoiled your plans."

"We can come back up and deal with those outlaws later," said Ben. "Don't you worry about it none. Like Dhu says, I ought to learn to keep my mouth shut sometimes."

"Yeah," said Dhu. "I really wish you would."

"Have you reported the robbery to the authorities?" Katharine asked.

"Well, no," said Ben. He didn't want to tell his sister that what was stolen from them was gold that might easily be considered to have been stolen in the first place.

"There's a problem in the Cherokee Nation," said Dhu, "in the whole so-called Indian Territory, with just who the authorities are. You see, the U.S. government won't allow Indians to arrest white people.

And these men are white. The only thing we could do is ride over into Arkansas and report it to the federal marshal's office. And that's a little out of the way. We'll take care of it ourselves, sooner or later."

It was nearly noon the next day when they drove the wagon up to the home of Ready Ballard. Ballard's was practically on the way, and Dhu figured it would be a good place to rest for a while. He knew, too, that they would get a good meal from Ballard. Ballard had heard their approach, and he was standing out in front of his cabin when they arrived.

" '*Siyo*, Dhu," he said. "Hello, Ben. Welcome back."

"Ready," said Dhu, "this is Katharine Lacey, Ben's sister. Katharine, this is a friend of mine, Ready Ballard."

"How do you do, Mr. Ballard?" said Katharine.

"Just fine, thank you," said Ready. "It's a pleasure meeting you. Let me help you down. All of you come on in the house."

They ate, and then they sat outside under the shade trees with cups of coffee. The afternoon was pleasant, not too hot, not cold.

"It's a nice day," said Katharine.

"Yes," said Ballard, "it is."

"And this is a beautiful country you have here."

"We like it," said Ballard. "It's a lot like our old country."

"We just hope we can hang onto it," said Dhu, but he was immediately sorry for having said it. There was no purpose served in trying to lay a burden of guilt on the shoulders of Ben and Katharine. And besides, he asked himself, if he was so concerned, why was he living in Texas and chasing after gold bars? Why wasn't he home fighting for the rights of the Cherokee Nation and the Cherokee people?

A few moments of silence followed. When Ballard saw that all of the coffee cups were empty, he went inside for the pot. He brought it back outside and refilled the cups. The pot was about empty then, so he put it on the ground and sat back down.

"Middle Striker was by here last night," he said. "He had some news for you."

Dhu glanced at Ben and then at Katharine. He had an idea what the news was about, but then, Ben had already let the story slip to Katharine about the robbery, so what the hell? Let him tell it.

"What news?" he asked.

"The Border Rats are holed up at Boyd Carr's place over in Arkansas," said Ballard.

"Are they still there?" said Dhu.

"Yeah. When Middle Striker came here to tell me, he left Bear-at-Home there to watch. If they leave that place, we'll know about it. One or the other of them will come around to tell us."

"Well," said Dhu, "our plans have changed just a bit. We have to get Katharine safely down to Texas. Then we'll come back and look for those Border Rats."

"They could be long gone by then," said Ballard. "And so could your money, too."

"We'll just have to take that chance," said Dhu.

"Why?" said Katharine. "Is there some place I could stay while you settle this business?"

"You could stay right here," said Ballard. "You're welcome. I'll ask my sister to come over and stay with us so you won't be alone here with just me."

"Oh, I wouldn't want to put you out," said Katharine. "Please. I wasn't fishing for an invitation. I thought there might be a hotel somewhere near. I —"

"You're welcome here," said Ballard.

Katharine looked at Dhu.

"Well?" she said.

Dhu looked at Ben, and Ben shrugged.

"Well," said Dhu, "in that case, I guess you can stay here for a while. We ought to be able to get this other business taken care of pretty quickly."

"Good," said Katharine. "It's settled then."

And Susie Anna Ballard did come. She was there the next morning. She was a short woman with a happy, round face and gray hair. She was older than Ready, and she used her age and sex to her advantage. She was a Cherokee matron, and she was in charge when she was around. But she managed to take charge without offending anyone. The Cherokees were not offended, because it was the Cherokee way. The Cherokees had always had matrilineal clans with clan matrons. Ben and Katharine were not offended because of Susie Anna's generally winning ways, her sunny disposition, and her obvious genuine concern for the feelings and the needs of all those around her. So with Susie Anna in the house, there was nothing more to keep Ben and Dhu from their business with the Border Rats. Everything was settled. Almost everything.

Chapter 15

Nebo Drake was standing on the porch in front of his house when Dhu arrived.

"Howdy," he said. "I been kind of looking for you." He turned his head to the left and spat a stream of brown tobacco juice.

"Oh?" said Dhu. "How come?"

"Just have been," said Drake. "That's all. Climb down out of that saddle and come on in. We'll have us a little drink of good brown whiskey."

Dhu dismounted, tied his horse, and followed Drake inside. They sat across from each other at a table with a dusty top, and Drake poured two glasses of whiskey. The glasses were dirty. He shoved one toward Dhu, and Dhu took it and drank it down. Drake drank his own down and refilled the glasses.

"What can I do for you?" said Drake. He turned his head and spat on the floor. Dhu wondered how the man drank whiskey with a chaw in his mouth. "You bring me any goods?"

"No," said Dhu. "I didn't bring anything this trip."

"Well, what is this? A business trip or a social call?"

"Neither one exactly," said Dhu. "I came looking for information."

Drake tipped up his glass and drank again. He poured himself another drink. Dhu hadn't yet touched his second one.

"What kind of information?" said Drake. "Talk's cheap today. Especially for an old friend and a good customer."

"You bought any gold lately?" asked Dhu. "Gold bars?"

"Could be," said Drake. "You got a reason for asking?"

"I was on my way up here with some business for you," said Dhu, "me and my partner, when we ran into an ambush. The bushwhackers got away with our pack-horse. Somebody told me it sounded like the Border Rats. I'm looking for them."

"The Border Rats don't come around here," said Drake. He spat and took another drink of whiskey, and then he paused, seemingly for effect. "But Boyd Carr does — every now and then. He come by here not too long ago. Had some gold bars. I took them off his hands."

Drake took a pencil stub out of his pocket, licked the lead, and scrawled some figures on a piece of paper which was there on the table. He shoved the paper toward Dhu, digging a furrow in the dust, and Dhu took it and read it.

"That's what I give him for it," said Drake.

"You'd have given me about two thousand more than that," said Dhu, "unless the price of gold has dropped since I was here last."

"It ain't," said Drake. "But he ain't you, and I ain't never liked that slick skunk no how. I thought that might have been your stuff he had there, but I couldn't be sure of it, you know. I damn sure couldn't figure out a way that little bastard could have got anything away from you. The Border Rats, huh? Well, I can't pay you back for what I give him, but I can make out in my books like I done business with you and give you the difference."

Drake went into the back room. When he reemerged, he had a handful of bills. He tossed them on the table in front of Dhu, and a puff of dust rose up around them.

"There," he said. "Now I've paid your full price. I just didn't give it all to you direct, that's all. But if you catch up with Carr or with them Border Rats, well, now you know just how much they owe you."

"I know," said Dhu, "and I will catch up with them."

Back at Ready Ballard's house, Dhu paced the floor. "I always figured there was something wrong at Boyd Carr's place," he said. "It's a haven for outlaws, including the Border Rats, and he helps them get rid of their ill-gotten gains. I always have suspected him of something. That's why I didn't hesitate to steal his horses that time."

"When?" said Ben.

"That's where we stole those horses right after we escaped from the rebs," said Dhu.

"Oh," said Ben. "Yeah. I remember. That was just over in Arkansas. Right?"

"Right. Just across the line." Dhu turned toward Ballard. "Any more word from Middle Striker?"

"Nothing new," said Ballard. "I figure that means the Border Rats are still there at Carr's place. If they had left, Middle Striker would be here to tell us."

"Then what I need to do," said Dhu, "is to get on over there and look the place over and figure out how to attack that gang."

"What do you mean?" said Ben. "Don't you mean, 'what we need to do'?"

"No, Ben. I mean just what I said. If anything goes wrong, I don't want Katharine to be left here without an escort on down to the ranch. I'll tackle this one alone."

"I'd think that maybe I would have something to say about that," said Katharine. "I certainly don't want you taking extra risks just because of my presence here."

"I've made up my mind," said Dhu. "Don't worry. I'll be extra careful."

He didn't say the rest of what was on his mind. He didn't tell Katharine that he would be especially careful because he wanted to see her again. But that was just what he was thinking. Then he said to himself, how in the world did Ben Lacey ever get a sister as pretty as that?

Dhu had been gone maybe ten minutes when Katharine walked over to Ben and looked him in the eyes.

"Ben," she said, "I know what he said, but go after him. I wouldn't want anything to happen to him because of me."

"But he was right, Sis," said Ben. "I mean, we can take care of ourselves pretty good, me and Dhu, especially Dhu, but you never know. What if something did happen to both of us out there? How would you get on down to the ranch?"

"I've got money," said Katharine. "I'm sure that I could arrange for transportation somewhere. I'd go to Preston. Right?"

"Well, yeah, but . . ."

"We could arrange it," said Ballard. "Don't worry. Go after him, my friend."

"And I'll add another voice to that if we're voting on it," said Susie Anna, who had kept quiet so far. "We're all right here, but Dhu Walker's riding into trouble. Go after him, Ben. The chances are a whole lot better if there's two of you. And if anything should go wrong, me and Ready, we'll take good care of Katharine. Don't you worry about that a bit."

Ben was outnumbered and outvoted. He saddled his horse and rode after Dhu. And really, he was glad to be going. He hadn't felt right about leaving the fighting to Dhu alone anyhow. And he was proud of his sister for having said what she did. She's got spunk, he said to himself. She sure does.

He didn't try to catch up. Rather he deliberately trailed behind Dhu. He didn't want to get into any arguments with his partner about this change in plans. Sometimes he could read Dhu's trail, and now and then when he found himself on high ground, he could even spot Dhu up ahead. He kept moving slow and easy, just making sure that he kept Dhu in sight or at least within easy reach. Because of the sun, he was aware that they were traveling east.

As he rode along, he thought about Dhu Walker, a man he had not liked at first, a man who could still irritate him more than almost any other human being he had ever known. Yet Dhu was probably the best friend Ben had ever had. And he sure didn't want anybody shooting at Dhu if he wasn't around to help shoot back.

Newt Trainor had decided that it would be a sin and a shame to leave Boyd Carr's place right away with so much good whiskey and food in stock, so he had told the Border Rats that they would hole up there for a while and use up the stores. Billy Bardette had protested a little bit. There were no women at the place. But none of the Border Rats ever protested too long or too hard over a decision Trainor had made. They just accepted it. And so they lounged around and ate and drank. Eli Turnbull had searched the place diligently looking for something to read. He found nothing.

"What the hell kind of illiterate son of a bitch was he anyhow?" he asked.

"What did you call him?" said Murv.

"A son of a bitch," said Eli.

"No, hell," said Murv. "I know what a son of a bitch is. I mean that other word you said."

"Oh. Illiterate?"

"Yeah," said Murv. "That one. What's that mean?"

"It means the dumb bastard couldn't read or write," said Eli. "That's what the hell it means."

"Oh."

Dhu left his horse hidden in the trees and climbed on foot to the top of the rise overlooking the land of Boyd Carr. He had a good view of the house and the barn, but he couldn't really tell anything. He couldn't tell from looking down on the place if anyone was even there. He decided he would have to wait for dark and move down to get a better look. He settled down there on the hill to wait and to watch.

Ben found Dhu's horse. He climbed down out of the saddle and tied his own there beside it. Then he started looking around. It didn't take him long to locate

Dhu there where he was watching the Carr place. Ben recognized it as the very place he and Dhu had looked down from before. He thought about making his presence known to Dhu, about joining Dhu up there on the hill, but he decided to wait a while yet. He would wait until Dhu was ready for action. Then there would be no time for arguments. In the meantime, maybe he could learn something.

He mounted up again, and keeping as much as possible to cover, he rode a wide circle around the Carr property until he found himself behind the barn. Again he dismounted and tied his horse in the woods. He tried to see Dhu from this new location, but he couldn't. That probably meant that Dhu couldn't see him either. On foot, he made his way to the barn. He saw no one on the way.

Pressed against the barn wall, Ben eased himself to the corner and carefully peeked around the edge. He could see the house, but he could detect no movement, no signs of life. He went back around to the back of the barn and found a door there. He tried it, and it opened. He went inside. As soon as his eyes adjusted to the dimmer light, he began to look around. It was a fairly typical barn except for the closed-in room along one side. He sneaked a look into the long room and found that it was furnished like a bunkhouse. But no one was there. He went back out and checked the stalls along the other side of the barn. There were ten horses there in stalls. He wasn't at all sure what that meant.

He went back out the way he had come in, and went to the back corner of the barn to try for another look at the house. Still he could see no one, but just as he was about to leave, he heard a voice. It was loud and argumentative and it came from inside the house. He waited, but he never heard a response. At last he gave it up and made his way back to his horse in the woods.

The sun was getting low in the sky by this time, and Ben decided that he had better let Dhu know he was there. If he waited until dark, Dhu might shoot him by mistake. He rode back around to where Dhu's horse still waited patiently in the woods, and again he tied his own horse there. Then he started on foot up the back side of the rise where he had last seen Dhu.

"Dhu?" he said in a harsh whisper. "Dhu. Can you hear me?"

He reached the ridge without seeing anyone, and then Dhu stepped up behind him.

"What the hell are you doing here?"

"I'm here and that's that," said Ben. "If you want to argue about it, we'll argue later. I went down there and looked in the barn. There's horses there, but I didn't see no people. I heard a voice though. Someone kind of loud inside the house. But I couldn't see in, and I didn't hear no other voices."

"But if you heard one loud voice," said Dhu, "it's likely there was at least one other human being in there."

"Maybe," said Ben. "I've knowed men to yell pretty loud at their dogs."

"How many horses did you find in the barn?"

"There was ten or so," said Ben.

"Damn," said Dhu. "I believe the Border Rats are in there with Boyd Carr, but I'd sure like to know before I charge down there like a damn fool."

Katharine had stood for a long time in front of the house after Ben had ridden away. She stared off in the direction in which Dhu and then Ben had gone. At first Ready Ballard and his sister Susie Anna had left her alone, but Susie Anna at last decided that Katharine needed some company. She walked out to join her. Stepping up beside her, she put an arm around Katharine's shoulders.

"Try not to worry too much," she said. "I've known Dhu Walker for a long time, and I know for sure that he can take care of himself. And your brother Ben looks to me like he can do a pretty good job, too. Together they ought to be able to handle any gang of ruffians out there."

"What if Dhu gets there too far ahead of Ben?" said Katharine. "What if he really does have to fight them all by himself?"

Susie Anna gave Katharine a look of sudden realization, and she squeezed her shoulders. So, she thought, it's really Dhu she's worrying over. Well, I sure can't blame her for that. If I was a few years younger, I'd be fighting her over that boy.

"Katharine," she said, "they'll be all right. Both of them. Just you wait and see."

"Oh, Susie Anna," said Katharine, "I sure do hope you're right."

"Have you known me to be wrong yet?" said Susie Anna. "Come on. Let's go inside and have a nice, hot cup of coffee."

Chapter 16

"Dhu," said Ben, "how are we going to handle this? We don't know how many's in there? We don't even know who it is that's in there?"

"I think it's the Border Rats and Boyd Carr in there, Ben," said Dhu. "But you're right. We have to know before we do anything."

"Well, how're we going to find out? We can't just walk down there and knock on the door and ask them."

"No," said Dhu. "We can't do that. Or maybe we can — sort of."

He stood up and started walking down the hill toward where the horses were waiting, grazing contentedly. Ben, still sitting on the ground on top of the rise, turned to watch him.

"What are you up to?" he asked.

Dhu walked to his horse and withdrew the rifle from its sheath on the side of the saddle. He checked its load, then started back toward Ben. At the top of the rise, he dropped down on his stomach and leveled his rifle, aiming at the house.

"What're you doing?" said Ben. "Do you see anyone down there? I don't see no one, Dhu. What are you up to?"

"I'm going to knock on the door," said Dhu. He squeezed the trigger, and the rifle roared. An instant later, the lead smashed into the front door of Boyd Carr's house.

Inside the house, Newt Trainor jumped to his feet, revolver in hand. He ran to the front window and looked out, but he could see no one.

"Get up, you bastards," he yelled. "Get in here."

In another minute the Border Rats were gathered around Trainor. Trainor was still looking out the window.

"What was that?" asked Billy Bardette.

"Damn it, I don't know," said Trainor, "but someone's out there. He shot the goddamn door."

"The law?" said Murv.

"How the hell would I know," said Trainor. "Someone. Murv, take my place here at the window. Keep watching. If you see anything move out there, holler at me. And kill it. You hear?"

"Yeah," said Murv. "Sure."

Murv squatted down by the window, and Trainor stood up and moved to the middle of the room. The others waited for his orders.

"We need to know who's out there," he said, "and how many of them they is. We also need to keep a good watch to make sure they ain't sneaking in on us. I want someone looking out in every direction. Billy, you get over to that side window. Bobby, the other side. Eli, you take the back side of the house. Get going."

The Rats scattered, and Trainor stood alone in the middle of the room, gun in hand. He turned around in a circle, looking in all directions, trying to think, trying to make some kind of a decision. Who the hell could it be out there? he wondered. How many? And where could they be?

Up on the hillside, Ben and Dhu waited.

"What good did that do?" said Ben. "Now they know we're here."

"Now they'll do something," said Dhu.

"What? They ain't going to walk out the door so we can shoot them. Are they?"

"You talk too much, Ben," said Dhu. He finished reloading the rifle. "Go get your saddle gun. Six-guns are no good from this distance."

Ben ran down the hill for his own rifle,

still wondering just what Dhu had accomplished. He got the rifle and rejoined Dhu.

"All right," he said. "What now?"

"Just settle down here and watch," said Dhu, "and keep quiet if you can."

Newt Trainor found a gun cabinet in Carr's living room. Four rifles were in the cabinet. He loaded them all and took them, with extra ammunition, to the front window where Murv was watching.

"I ain't seen nothing yet, Newt," said Murv.

"Here," said Trainor, kneeling down beside Murv. "You take two of these, and I'll keep the other two."

Murv looked puzzled, but he took the two rifles Trainor shoved at him.

"I figure there's someone out there up on that rise," said Trainor. "I figure if we shoot at them, they'll shoot back. Maybe we can find out how many they are and just where they're at. Now, when I say go, start shooting. You ready?"

"Yeah. I'm ready."

The look Murv's face wore was eager.

"Then — go," said Trainor, and he pulled the trigger.

"Get down," said Dhu.

The rifle shot had hit the dirt just a few feet below them. They hunkered down on the back side of the rise, and three more rifle shots rang out. Then there was a pause.

"Give it back to them," said Dhu. "The window down there."

He fired at the window, and Ben fired immediately after. Then nothing more happened. They reloaded their rifles.

"Well," said Dhu, "we know there's more than one."

"Two shots back," said Trainor. "Two rifle shots. There's two of them, and they're up there on that rise, just out in front of us. Reload these rifles, and keep watching that rise."

"Yeah," said Murv. "Okay. I see anything move, I'll kill it." He began reloading as Trainor moved back.

"You do that," said Trainor. He stood up and walked to the back of the house. Eli Turnbull was there at the window looking out. He glanced over his shoulder when he heard Trainor's footsteps approaching.

"What's all the shooting up there, Newt?" he asked.

"Nothing," said Trainor. "It ain't important."

"Well, I ain't seen nothing out here."

"That's cause there ain't nothing to see," said Trainor. "They're out front. Two of them up on that rise out there. You know where I mean?"

"Yeah. I seen it. Just out front?"

"That's right. Now listen. I want you to go out the back here and then circle around. Keep to them trees until you get on the side of that rise. Get behind them and kill them. Murv'll keep their attention while you're getting into position. You got that?"

"Sure," said Turnbull.

"Them trees out there runs all the way around to the other side of that rise," said Trainor. "If you're careful, you can keep to cover the whole way. It'll just take you a little time. That's all."

"Sure," said Turnbull, checking the load in his second six-gun. "I'll go out here, get in the trees, and keep to them until I've worked my way around to the back side of the rise. It's a cinch, Newt. You can count on me."

"Good. Get going then and get it done."

Turnbull opened the door and looked out. Then he stepped outside, pulled the door shut behind himself, and was gone. Trainor started through the house. On his way he picked up Bardette and Brown.

"Go to the front window there and help Murv out," he said. "There's two men on the rise out there. Just keep their attention. That's all."

Turnbull raced from the house into the woods nearby. The going was much slower than he had anticipated, for the undergrowth was thick. He thought about getting out of the woods and walking along the edge, but he decided that would be too dangerous. It was important that he not be seen, and besides, Trainor had told him to go through the trees. So he stayed and fought his way through the tangled brush and bramble. Gnats swarmed around his head, and he was soon sweating in the heat. He nearly tripped and fell several times, and he was cursing under his breath.

"I'll kill them, all right," he said to himself, "and I'll like the hell out of it."

It took all of his attention to move through the woods. He had to look up to keep from running into trees, and he had to look down to watch where he was stepping. He had just stepped over some deadfall, and he raised his head to look forward again. There standing in front of him, blocking his path, holding an old .44

caliber revolver aimed at his chest, was a dark-skinned Indian. Turnbull opened his mouth in shocked surprise. He reached for the revolver hanging at his side. Middle Striker pulled the trigger, and there was a deafening roar, a cloud of blue smoke, and the air was filled with the acrid smell of burnt black powder. Overhead, birds twittered and flew, leaves rustled, and squirrels scolded and chattered. Turnbull stood for a moment, a stupefied expression on his face, as dark red blood came out in rhythmic spurts from the fresh hole in his chest. His arms dangled limply at his sides. He began to reel, and then he pitched forward to lie dead in the tangle on the forest floor.

"What was that?" said Ben.

"Seemed like it came from over there," said Dhu. "Almost behind the house."

"That don't make any sense," said Ben.

"I don't know," said Dhu. "Maybe it does. Keep your eyes on that window down there, Ben. If you see any movement, shoot."

Newt Trainor heard the shot too, and it worried him. It sounded to him like it was just outside, out to the side of the house, and he knew that it was too soon for Turnbull to have made it to the back side of the rise. What could it mean? There must be a third person out there somewhere, he reasoned. And either Turnbull had shot him, or he had shot Turnbull. Trainor decided that he couldn't just wait around to find out which way it had happened. He looked toward the front of the house. The rest of the Rats were at the front window where he had left them.

He glanced quickly around the room. There were all the saddlebags there. The Border Rats had been sleeping in the back room of the house, and all of their personal belongings were lying about in that room. He knew that each man had his share of the money stashed in his own saddlebags. It would be a shame to leave all that money to those dumb kids, he thought, especially if whoever was out there shooting happened to get them. Quickly, nervously, he gathered up all the money and stuffed it into his saddlebags, then hurried out the back door, watching over his shoulder.

Pressing against the back wall of the house, Trainor moved slowly to the corner and peered around. He could see no one, and he assumed that no one could see him. He ran to the barn and went in the back door. In a few moments, his horse was saddled and the money-filled saddlebags were secured. He led the horse to the big door at the front of the barn, kicked the door open, mounted up, and rode out, kicking and lashing at the horse in a fury that was near panic.

"Dhu, look," said Ben.

"I see him," said Dhu, and he took careful aim with his rifle and fired. "Missed him. Damn it."

Then the front door of the house opened, and the three remaining Border Rats came running out onto the porch.

"Hey," shouted Murv, looking after Trainor. "Where the hell are you going?"

Ben fired a rifle shot that tore a gash across Murv's thigh, and the Rats went back inside. They gathered up again at the window and fired a few rounds back toward Ben and Dhu.

"It's a goddamned Mexican standoff," said Bobby Brown.

"Where the hell is Newt going?" said Murv.

"I'll tell you in a minute," said Bardette. He ran through the house to the back room, looked around hurriedly, checking the saddlebags, then ran back again. "The son of a bitch took all the money," he said. "He's run out on us."

"Newt?" said Murv.

"He's gone, and the money's gone," said Bardette. "What's that sound like to you?"

"If I ever see him again, I'll kill him," said Murv. "I trusted him. I trusted him with my life. By God, I'll kill him for that."

"Not if I see him first," said Bardette. "Damn. All that money. He's got all our money."

"Well, what the hell are we going to do right now?" said Brown. "We sure ain't going to find Newt to kill him and to get back our money if we don't get out of here alive."

"He got out the back and got to a horse," said Bardette. "So can we."

"Ben," said Dhu, "it's too quiet down there. My guess is that they're all going to try for the horses."

"What do we do about it?" said Ben.

"Let's mount up," said Dhu. "You ride around to the right, and I'll go to the left. If they come riding out of that barn, we'll hit them from both sides."

"Let's go then," said Ben.

"You first," said Dhu. He watched the house while Ben ran down to the horses, mounted up, and started riding to the right. Then he, too, got up and ran for his horse.

Inside the barn the remaining Border Rats got their horses saddled and checked their weapons one last time. They gave each other stern determined looks and quick affirmative nods. Then they mounted up.

"You all ready?" said Bardette.

"Yeah," said Murv, wincing. "Let's go."

Bardette was the first one out the front barn door, and almost immediately, he saw Dhu Walker racing toward him. It was too late to turn around and go back inside, too late to change his mind. He jerked up his revolver and fired, but the shot went wide and wild. Dhu reined in his mount and jumped out of the saddle, pulling the rifle with him. He dropped to one knee, set the rifle to his shoulder, and squeezed off a round. Bardette jerked and fell out of the saddle, landing with a thud and bouncing in a cloud of dust.

Brown came out just behind Bardette, and when he saw what was happening, he jerked his reins to his left in an attempt to escape from Dhu. Then he saw that he was rushing toward Ben. Ben, sitting still in the saddle, aimed his rifle and fired. Brown screamed and fell backward, but his feet hung up in the stirrups. He lay dead across his horse's rump, and the animal ran. The lifeless body bounced like a rag doll.

Still inside the barn, red-haired Murv urged his horse backward. He had seen what had happened out there, and he wasn't about to rush into the same fate. But what would he do? By God, he'd fight it out with them right there, he decided. He dismounted awkwardly and slapped the horse on the rump. It ran free out the door. Ben and Dhu looked at each other, and Dhu waved with his gun hand toward the barn. Ben nodded. Both men rode toward it, one from each side. At the corners of the building, they dismounted. Each held a six-gun in his hand. Staying close to the wall they moved toward the door.

Murv was standing in the middle of the barn. His revolver was in his hand. Blood ran down his leg from the wound to his thigh. He was watching the door for any sign of the two men and was backing slowly toward the rear of the building. A shot rang out, and he felt something rip through his chest from the back. He looked down, and he saw the blood spurt. He felt his fingers grow weak, and he watched as they relaxed their grip on the revolver and let it fall to the floor. He felt dizzy, and then he felt nothing. He pitched forward to land on his face and to feel no more.

Behind the body stood Middle Striker, smoking .44 in his hand. It was quiet. This must be the last one, he thought. He took a deep breath and put an open hand to the side of his mouth.

"*Inoli,*" he called out, using Dhu Walker's Cherokee name.

Ben turned a questioning face toward Dhu, and he could see Dhu relax and then smile just a little.

"That's Middle Striker," Dhu said, and he called out something in Cherokee. Ben, of course, couldn't understand, but in a moment, Middle Striker stepped out to join them. They had won. They had wiped out the notorious Border Rats, all except Newt Trainor, and, by damn, Ben thought, we'll get him, too, I guess. He looked down again at the body close by, and he could remember the other one, the one he had shot.

"I don't feel too good about this, Dhu," he said.

"Why not?" asked Dhu.

"Killing folks like this. It don't feel good.

These guys are just hardly more than kids."

"Those guns and the way they used them made them men," said Dhu, "and besides that, if the United States government would allow it, we could have let the Cherokee Nation law handle it for us. The way things are, we only had two choices: either let them go and forget about it, or do what we did."

Ben heaved a deep sigh.

"Yeah," he said. "I guess you're right. Hell, you usually are. Well, let's go get that other bastard then."

Chapter 17

Checking the bodies, they found Billy Bardette still alive. He was hurt bad, and they didn't think that he would last much longer, but he was conscious. Dhu knelt beside the wounded outlaw.

"You've killed me, you son of a bitch," said Bardette.

"It looks that way," said Dhu.

"Did you get Newt?" Bardette asked, his voice a raspy whisper.

"Newt Trainor?" said Dhu.

"Yeah. Him. He run out on us, the dirty bastard. We never thought he'd do that. Took all the money, too."

Bardette coughed and spit up some blood that ran down his chin and onto his neck. Dhu thought that he would go right then, but the fit subsided, and Bardette took a few breaths before he tried to speak again.

"Get the son of a bitch," he said.

"Do you have any idea where he might go?" said Dhu.

"Not for sure," said Bardette. "He'd been talking lately about Texas. Get him.

Will you? The dirty son of a bitch."

"I mean to," said Dhu. "Tell me Where's Boyd Carr?"

"Huh? Oh. Old Boyd," said Bardette. His lips curled momentarily into a half smile, and he coughed again. "I damn near forgot about old Boyd. Newt killed him. We throwed his body out in the woods for the hogs."

Then Bardette surprised Dhu. There were no more coughing fits. He just closed his eyes, and he was dead.

Newt Trainor could hear the shooting behind him as he rode away, and when he heard no more, he knew that someone would be after him and soon. If the Border Rats had killed the attackers, they would come after him for running out on them with all the money. That didn't bother him much. He figured he could handle them. He always had before. He would just tell them that his plan had worked. They were safe, the money was safe, and the attackers were dead. Then he would tell them to ride on down to Texas with him, and everything would be just fine. He could tell them anything and make them believe it. He hoped that they had won the fight. He figured that they had. Those boys were a ough bunch. They'd be hard to kill. But ae didn't know who the other guys were.

If the other guys had won, it would be a lifferent situation. He didn't even know who they were, but he now thought that there were three of them. He was pretty sure that there had been two on the hill out front, and then there had been a shot from the woods to the side of the house, and Eli had not been heard of since. There must have been a third one out in the woods. So if they had won the fight back at Carr's, they would be after him. He didn't think it was the law. The law would usually identify themselves, wouldn't they? Didn't they usually give folks a chance to surrender before they started shooting? He wondered who those guys were.

Well, by God, he would find out, and pretty damn soon. He decided to look for a good spot for an ambush. He would stop, hide his horse, and watch the trail. If his own boys came along, then he would hail them and talk them out of being mad at him. If it was anyone else, he would shoot first and ask questions later.

Dhu, Ben, and Middle Striker made a quick search of Boyd Carr's house and the surrounding area. They found Carr's remains in the woods nearby. They found their own packhorse in the barn, but they found no money anywhere. Everything seemed to confirm the dying words of Billy Bardette.

Dhu had a brief conversation in Cherokee with Middle Striker, then he turned to Ben.

"Let's go get our horses," he said. "We've let him get too much of a start on us already."

"What about him?" said Ben, nodding toward Middle Striker.

"He's going with us," said Dhu.

Ben and Dhu ran up and over the hilltop to the place in the woods where their horses waited. They mounted up and rode back over the rise. Middle Striker was there already, on horseback and waiting for them. The three of them then started after Trainor. He had ridden out going north.

"This ain't the way to Texas," said Ben.

"No," said Dhu, "but it's the way he went."

They rode on for several minutes, the urgency of their mission held in check by caution. They watched the tracks that Trainor had left to make sure that he hadn't gone off the trail somewhere, and they watched the trail ahead as much as possible in anticipation of an ambush. They knew from experience that Trainor wouldn't hesitate to shoot from hiding. When the sun was about to go down behind the trees, they had not yet come across Trainor. His trail was still clear, but they couldn't tell how far ahead he might be.

"We'll have to stop pretty soon," said Dhu. "We can't track him after dark. We can't spot an ambush either."

"He could keep traveling after dark though," said Ben. "If he rides all night, we might not ever catch him."

"If he tries to ride all night," Dhu said, "he'll kill his horse. He may ride into the night some, but I don't think he'll ride all night. We'll catch up."

They found a stream and made a camp beside it. They decided that a small fire wouldn't really be much of a risk. After all, they were following Trainor, not the other way around. So they boiled some coffee and drank it. Middle Striker went to his saddlebags and produced a ball of something. He held it up with a smile. Dhu returned the smile.

"Ah," he said, *"kanutche. Osd'. Agiyosiduh."*

"What's that?" said Ben.

"Just what I said. *Kanutche,*" said Dhu.

"Food. We won't have to sleep on empty stomachs."

"Well, what is it?" said Ben. "That — what you said."

"Just pounded up hickory nuts," said Dhu. "That's all."

"Then mashed into that big ball?"

"Yeah."

"What'd you call it?" said Ben.

"Never mind," said Dhu. "Just eat it."

Middle Striker got a pot out of his saddlebags and took it to the stream for water. Then he put it on the fire to boil. He put the kanutche ball into the water, and before long he had a thick, hot broth. He spoke in Cherokee to Dhu.

"Middle Striker says we'll have to take it straight this time," said Dhu. "Sometimes we cook meat or corn or rice or something in with it. It's a little rich like this, but it will fill us up all right."

Ben thought about refusing his share, but his stomach was growling, and he was afraid that Dhu and Middle Striker had already heard it. So if he refused the stuff, they'd know why. He thought he wouldn't like it, though, and when he tasted it, at first he thought he had been right. But he surprised himself by getting used to it, and before he had finished, he had decided that t was not bad at all. Really, he thought, it was pretty good. And his stomach sure felt better. He was glad that Middle Striker had brought it along. Hickory nuts. He couldn't remember what Dhu had called it. Mashed hickory nuts.

"I don't believe there's any real danger," said Dhu, "but just to be sure, I think one of us ought to stay awake. I'll take the first watch."

Ben didn't have to wait long before dropping off into a deep and restful sleep. He dreamed of Iowa cornfields and of beautiful horses on a ranch in Texas, and he dreamed of beautiful girls. One of them was his wife, one was his sister. The third was his two-year-old daughter. Then he felt someone shaking his shoulder, and he was awake all too soon.

"Your turn, Ben," said Dhu. "In a couple of hours, wake up Middle Striker."

"All right," said Ben. He rubbed his eyes, trying to clear his head, and Dhu handed him a cup of hot coffee. "Oh, thanks," he said. "That'll help."

"Sit back over there," said Dhu. "Back from the fire. That way you won't make a target for anyone who might come along."

"Yeah," said Ben.

Dhu crawled into his bedroll, and Ben

found himself a tree trunk to lean back on away from the fire. He sat down and sipped his coffee. He sure did hope that this business would be over and done with early in the morning. He wanted to get back to his sister and hurry on back to Texas. He wanted to see Mary Beth, and he wanted to hold Nellie Bell in his arms.

When he thought that the two hours was about up, he stood up, stretched, and walked over to Middle Striker's bedroll. There was no one there. He knelt beside the blanket. He looked around. He could not see Middle Striker anywhere. He moved over to where the horses had been hobbled for the night, and there were only two.

"Damn," he said. He hurried to Dhu and shook him awake.

"What?" said Dhu. "What is it?"

"Middle Striker's gone," said Ben. "He's gone and his horse is gone. I didn't see nothing, Dhu, and I didn't hear nothing. I wasn't asleep either. I swear to God, I been wide awake the whole damn time."

Dhu tossed his blanket aside, got up on his feet, and started looking around.

"I never went to sleep," said Ben.

"Calm down, Ben," said Dhu. "I believe you. If Middle Striker wanted to slip away from you or me, he'd do it. That's all. And us never the wiser. Well, I'm awake now. You might as well go ahead and get some more sleep."

"But where'd he go?" said Ben. "He wouldn't run out on us, would he?"

"I don't know where he went," said Dhu, "but wherever it was, he had his reasons. Don't worry about it."

In the morning they had some coffee, nothing else. They wanted to get back on the trail as quickly as possible. They saw no sign of Middle Striker or his horse. He seemed to have left no tracks, no trace. It was as if he had never been there with them at all, except for the blanket that he had left on the ground.

The trail that Newt Trainor had taken out of Boyd Carr's place had gone north for a few miles, then turned west. In another few miles it ran into the old Texas Road and ended there, forming a T. Just across the Texas Road from the end of the trail stood an old and gnarled red oak tree. The old oak had a distinct list to the north, so much so that its large roots on the southern side were raised up from the ground. Behind the largest of these exposed roots, Newt Trainor lay on his belly, two revolvers and a rifle on the ground beside him. He could shoot under the big root or over it. It was a good spot, providing good cover. His horse was hidden in the trees on the opposite side of the road. He had decided to wait for whoever was on his trail. It was a warm day, but his belly was full of food and water, he had good shade, and he didn't think that he would have to wait too much longer for his pursuers to arrive. He could take it.

Dhu Walker made a gesture toward Ben Lacey indicating that he wanted to stop. Ben read it right, and they both hauled back on the reins. Ben gave Dhu a questioning look, but for once he kept quiet. Dhu pointed straight ahead on the trail. Then he spoke to Ben in a voice that was little more than a whisper.

"That's the end of the trail up there," he said. "It runs right into the Texas Road. Right there. Now, Trainor had to do one of three things. He either turned north or turned south or he's still there at the crossroads."

"What are we going to do?" said Ben.

"Come on," said Dhu, and he turned his mount and rode off the trail into the trees.

Ben followed, and they dismounted. "You stay here with the horses. I'm going to do a little investigating."

Dhu began walking through the woods toward the Texas Road. He moved slowly, staying as quiet as he could. As he drew closer to the road, he eased the six-gun out of its holster and held it ready. Then an unexpected noise caused his heart to jump. He recovered himself quickly. It had been a horse's nicker — close by. He eased on ahead, and then he saw it. It was tied there in the trees. It must be Trainor's mount, he thought, and that means that Trainor is somewhere near. He patted the horse on the side to reassure it and, he hoped, to keep it quiet, then he moved up closer to the road for a better look. He thought about checking the saddlebags, but he didn't know where Trainor was, and he didn't want to take a chance on Trainor's getting the drop on him while he was distracted with something else. He decided it would wait.

He could see the road, but he saw no sign of Trainor. Of course, he told himself, the man could be anywhere in the trees, just waiting for them to come riding by. Then he noticed the big oak across the road. He looked at it for some time, suspiciously. Still he saw no sign of Trainor. He was about to turn around and make his way back to Ben when he saw a movement, brief and small, almost imperceptible. He stared at the tree for a long moment after, but he saw nothing more. He could have been mistaken. He waited.

Ben jerked out his revolver and turned quickly to face the noise he heard coming up behind him, and then he saw that it was Dhu returning from his trip through the woods.

"What'd you find?" he asked.

"I can't be sure, Ben," said Dhu, "but I know he's up there somewhere. I found his horse hidden in the woods. You see that big red oak tree straight ahead?"

"Yeah."

"I think he's waiting for us right there."

"Behind that tree?"

"That's my guess."

"You didn't see him?"

"No. I said I can't be sure. I just think that's where he's waiting. And there's no way we can get around behind him without being seen. If he's there, he's got a clear view of the road in both directions."

"So what's our next move?"

Dhu shook his head. "I don't know," he said.

"Well, damn it, Dhu," said Ben, "we've got to do something, even if it's wrong."

"If it's wrong, Ben," said Dhu, "it'll kill us. Let's sit down and think this thing over, pard."

Chapter 18

Thane Savage could stand it no longer. The hate was building up to an explosive point, and he had to have some action. He talked three more Meriwether hands into riding along with him to the LWM. All four men were armed with six-guns. On their way, they stopped in Preston to drink some whiskey. The whiskey bolstered their spirits and added a hard edge to their already existing mean streak. When they rode through the big gate at the LWM and on down the path to the main house, Herd McClellan stepped out onto his front porch with a double-barreled shotgun in his hands. He recognized the Meriwether hands, although he did not know them by name. He raised the barrel of the shotgun, pointing it in the general direction of Savage's chest.

"What's your business here?" he demanded.

"We come to see Sam Ed," said Savage.

"What about?"

"That's between me and him."

"Sam Ed's my boy," said Herd. "Any business you got with him is my business.

Now I ain't going to ask you again."

"Listen, old man," said Savage, "you can't take us all out, not even with that scattergun."

As Savage spoke, the riders on either side of him began moving to the sides, spreading out. Their hands moved tentatively to the butts of their revolvers.

"Maybe not," said Herd, keeping the shotgun pointed casually at Savage, "but I'll damn sure get you."

"And we'll get the rest," came a voice from behind the Meriwether riders.

Savage turned his head slowly to look over his shoulder and saw Sam Ed and Charlie Bair standing there, each with a revolver in his hand.

"Now," said Herd, "you can either ride back out of here, or you can reach for those guns — and die. It's your choice."

"Wait a minute, Papa," said Sam Ed. "Savage, what's this all about?"

"You and me," said Savage. "I come over here to settle this thing between us once and for all."

"With guns?" asked Sam Ed.

"Any way you want it."

"That sounds all right to me, but there ain't no reason to involve all these other people in our fight, is there?" said Sam Ed.

"I don't need no help, but I don't want nobody shooting me in the back, and I don't want no one helping you fight me."

"Then, by God," said Sam Ed, "let's settle it. Papa and Charlie will stay out of it if your pals will."

"Boys," said Savage, "nobody raise a hand, no matter what happens. You got that?"

"That's fine with us," said one of the cowboys. "I guess it never was our fight anyhow."

Savage swung down out of the saddle, and Sam Ed was unbuckling his gun belt.

"So you want it like that?" said Savage. He took off his own gun belt and handed it to the nearest cowboy. "Hold on to that for me," he said. Then he turned to face Sam Ed again, and he raised his fists up in front of his face. "Come on, boy," he said. "I'm going to whip your ass."

Just then Maude came out on the porch, and across the way, Mary Beth stepped out her own front door. For an instant, Maude looked as if she was going to say something, but a glance from Herd kept her quiet. Mary Beth had a towel in her hands, which she was wringing nervously.

"You can try," said Sam Ed. "But we got

an agreement, right? This ends it, one way or the other."

"Yeah," said Savage. "This ends it."

Savage took a couple of running steps toward Sam Ed and swung his right, but Sam Ed, stepping back, easily warded off the blow. Then he shot out a quick, sharp left jab that brought blood trickling out of the corner of Savage's mouth. Savage shook his head and glared at Sam Ed. He wiped the blood from his face with his left sleeve. Then he stepped in toward Sam Ed again, and again Sam Ed hit him with a left. Savage stepped back and spit blood.

"Damn you," he said.

"You ain't had enough already, have you?" said Sam Ed, fists poised for another attack.

Savage rushed at Sam Ed, but Sam Ed stepped aside and caught Savage on the side of the head with a hard right, and Savage sprawled in the dirt on his face.

"Come on," said Sam Ed. "Get up unless you're ready to quit. Come on."

Savage turned and sat up. As he did, his right hand found a smooth, round stone, a little smaller than fist size. He closed his hand around the stone, as he turned his body to the right, getting up on his right knee and left foot, preparing to stand. But then as he stood, he swung his right and hurled the stone. It struck Sam Ed just above the right eye, bouncing off with a sickening thud. Sam Ed staggered. Blood ran down through his eye, and a knot rose quickly where the stone had struck him. He felt stunned, dizzy, and his vision was blurred.

Savage was on his feet fast, and he was pounding Sam Ed with blows to the body. Sam Ed doubled over, his arms up to protect his face and head. Close in and hovering over him, Savage battered his rib cage from the sides. Sam Ed took the blows for a while, gathering his wits and gauging Savage's position. Then he quickly straightened up, the back of his skull catching Savage sharply under the chin, splitting the flesh and almost baring the bone. Savage's head snapped back, as Sam Ed stood up straight and drove a right hard and deep into Savage's midsection. He followed that with a left and then another right. Savage doubled over, the wind all pounded out of his lungs. His face was an unnatural blue.

Nellie Bell came out the front door of her house, and Mary Beth picked her up quickly to take her back inside.

"What are they doing?" said Nellie Bell.

"I want to see," but the door was shut on her protests.

"Finish it off, boy," shouted Herd.

Sam Ed reached down and took hold of Savage's shirt front. He pulled Savage up straight and hit him with a hard right cross. Savage fell to the ground, his face red and puffy and smeared with blood.

"Come on, Thane," said a cowboy. "Let's go. He's whipped you fair and square."

"No," said Savage. He struggled to get to his feet, but his knees buckled, and he fell again.

"Give it up, Savage," said Sam Ed.

Savage tried again. This time he managed to get to a standing position, but he stood unsteady, reeling.

"Come on, you bastard," he said, and red saliva sprayed from between his pulpy lips.

Sam Ed looked around at the various bystanders and gave a shrug. Then he hit Savage with a roundhouse right that knocked him underneath the horse of the nearest Meriwether ranch hand. The horse nickered and pranced and came close to stepping on the writhing form beneath it. The cowboy managed to get him under control again. Disgusted, he dismounted and took hold of Savage by an arm, dragging the limp puncher to his feet.

"Come on, Thane," he said. "You're whipped, and we're leaving."

"No," said Savage.

"You made a deal, Thane," said the cowboy, "and you made us a part of it. Now, by God, you stick to it. Come on."

With the cowboy's help, Savage stood, and the cowboy helped him over to his own mount. Savage took hold of the saddle horn, but the puncher had to push on his rump to help him swing up into the saddle. For a moment after that, Savage sat swaying on the back of his horse.

"All right," he said, panting. "All right, damn it. It's over. It's done. Let's get the hell out of here."

Then Savage, managing somehow to stay in his saddle, and the other Meriwether cowboys turned their horses around and rode out of the yard and away from the LWM. Sam Ed, hurt only where the stone had struck him, walked over to the water pump to wash his face.

Herd McClellan shook his head slowly.

"That's one tough youngster you raised there, Maude," he said.

Maude turned to go back inside. She didn't bother giving Herd even a glance as she responded to his comment, her voice dry, her tone matter-of-fact.

"There ain't none better," she said.

"I don't know, Dhu," said Ben. "It sounds kind of chancy to me."

"You have another idea?" said Dhu. "I'll listen if you have."

"No, I don't, but what if he ain't behind that tree? What if he's back there in the woods somewhere? While we're trying to slip up on him, he could be slipping up on one of us."

"That's why we have to be careful," said Dhu. "Well?"

"Well, hell, all right," said Ben. "Let's go get it done. I sure hope we don't get ourself killed though."

They separated, Dhu on the left side of the path and Ben on the right, and they made their way through the woods until they were in their positions at the edge of the Texas Road. The big oak was just across the road from them. Ben aimed his rifle at the oak and waited. He expected that Dhu was also in position, but he intended to wait for Dhu to make the first move. After all, it was Dhu's crazy idea. It seemed to Ben like a long wait, but at last he heard Dhu's voice call out.

"Trainor," said Dhu, his voice loud and clear. "Trainor. Are you there?"

"What if I am?" said Trainor. "Who the hell are you? Are you the law?"

"I'm here to collect some money you owe me, Trainor," said Dhu. "You throw the money out, and you can ride on. We'll just forget about the bullet you put in me. That's the best deal I have to offer."

"Who are you?" yelled Trainor. "I don't owe no money to nobody. What the hell are you talking about?"

"I'm talking about a stolen packhorse," said Dhu, "and what was on his back."

"The Indian?" said Trainor. "You the Indian?"

"Throw out the money and ride on," said Dhu.

"I figured you was dead," said Trainor, and he laughed. "I didn't think I'd be hearing from you again. It's them gold bars you're after, ain't it? Well, I ain't got them no more, so you can just forget it."

"You've got the money," said Dhu. "Toss it out."

"Why should I? Hell, you stole them gold bars yourself. I ain't stupid. If you didn't steal them yourself, you'd have the law after me."

"That's enough talk, Trainor," said Dhu. "Where are you?"

Dhu stood up just long enough for Trainor to get a look. Then he stepped behind a tree.

"I'm right over here," he said, and he fired a pistol shot at the oak tree. Trainor fired back with his rifle, then tossed it aside and stood up with a revolver in each hand. He fired two shots from each revolver in Dhu's direction. He was turned slightly to his own right, all his attention on Dhu, so Ben, coming from Trainor's left and behind him, stood up and ran across the road. He came up behind Trainor with his rifle ready.

"Trainor," he said, "drop your guns."

Trainor spun around and fired a wild shot, and Ben pulled the trigger. The rifle ball tore into Trainor's gut. Trainor grimaced in pain and staggered, firing both of his revolvers, one after the other into the dirt. He tried to raise his arms to aim at Ben, but the strength was draining out of him fast. He couldn't manage it. Then he dropped heavily to his knees. Ben walked over close, pulling out his revolver as he walked. Dhu was coming up from the other direction. Trainor looked up to see who had shot him, and he recognized Ben.

His face registered surprise along with the pain that was already there.

"Ioway?" he said. "You? You got me?"

His face took on a blank expression, his eyes glazed over, and he pitched forward, the top of his head striking the ground first. His back arched once, then his whole body sagged in death. Ben stood for a moment looking at the body.

"At least this one was a little older than the others," he said.

"I'll check his pockets," said Dhu. "You see what's in his saddlebags. His horse is just over there."

As Ben headed for the horse in the woods across the road, Dhu rolled the body of Newt Trainor over on his back. He found a little money in the pockets, but not much. Stuffing it in his own pocket, he walked toward Ben.

"Hey, Ben," he called. "You find it?"

"There ain't no money here," said Ben. "There ain't nothing in these saddlebags."

Puzzled, Dhu hurried on over to where Ben stood by the abandoned horse and searched the saddlebags again. Ben quietly resented that action, his face burning just a little.

"I told you," he said. "It ain't here. What'd you find over there — on him?"

Dhu pulled the few bills back out of his pocket and handed them to Ben.

"Just this," he said. "Where could it be? He had to have it when he left Carr's place. That one back there told us that Trainor took it, and we didn't find it any-place around Carr's."

"Could he have hid it somewhere along the way?" asked Ben.

"Why?" said Dhu. "If he was leaving the country, he'd want to take all the money along with him. Besides, I don't think he had time, with us right behind him."

Dhu walked out into the road scratching his head, and Ben followed him. They stood there for a moment in puzzled si-lence. Then Ben looked up and squinted his eyes, studying a far-off form on the road to the south.

"Look," he said. "Someone's coming."

For a few moments, the approaching rider was just a silhouette, and he was moving slowly and casually. They stood waiting for him to come closer.

"You sure we got them all?" asked Ben. "I wonder who that is."

Dhu didn't answer. He just stood and watched as the rider came closer and closer. Then at last he spoke.

"That's Middle Striker," he said.

In no hurry, Middle Striker rode nonchalantly on up to join the other two men. He swung his right leg over his horse's neck, slipped his left foot out of the stirrup, and dropped lightly to the ground. He smiled and nodded a greeting toward Ben and Dhu. Then he reached into his shirt front and pulled out a great wad of bills, which he held out toward Dhu, and then he said something in Cherokee. Dhu answered him, and Middle Striker spoke again. Again Dhu responded. Ben was getting impatient by this time.

"What the hell's going on?" he said.

"He stole our money from Trainor," said Dhu. "He said he wasn't sure we were going to be able to kill that man."

When they rode up to Ready Ballard's house, Ballard was already standing outside and waving a greeting. Susie Anna stepped out of the house to stand beside him, and then Katharine came running out the front door to meet them. As soon as Ben had dismounted, she threw her arms around his neck.

"Oh, I'm glad you're back," she said. "I was worried the whole time you were gone."

"I didn't mean to worry you, Sis. You

didn't seem too worried when we left," said Ben. "I figured you knew we could take care of ourselves."

"Men don't know nothing you don't tell them," said Susie Anna, "and they sure can't take care of themselves."

"Well, I was worried. I just didn't want you to know about it. That's all. Is it all over with?"

"Yeah. It's all over," said Ben. "We, uh, we done what we set out to do."

Katharine turned to face Dhu. He was dismounted by this time. She looked at him for a moment.

"I was worried about you, too," she said.

"Thank you," said Dhu, taking off his hat and nodding slightly. "I'm honored by your concern."

"Well, come on inside and eat then," said Susie Anna. "Then you all can rest up. I know you've had a hard ride, and you've got a long trip ahead of you yet."

The next morning, rested and well fed and once again provisioned for the trail, Ben and Dhu and Katharine were ready to head south. Dhu had paid Ready Ballard and Middle Striker handsomely for their services, in spite of their protests that he didn't need to do that.

"You know," he said, "somebody could take a ride over into Arkansas, too, and claim the reward for those Border Rats, if he had a mind to."

"Somebody just might do that," said Ballard.

"Mr. Ballard," said Katharine, "I can't thank you enough for your hospitality. You've been awfully good to me. And you, Susie Anna. You've been wonderful."

"Oh," said Susie Anna, "we didn't do nothing."

"Your company was thanks enough, Miss Lacey," said Ballard. "If you ever travel this way again, I hope you'll stop for a visit."

"You can count on that," said Katharine. "I could never come anywhere near here and not take the opportunity to visit such good friends."

"Well," said Dhu, "these horses are ready to go, and it's a long ways yet to Texas. We'd better hit the road."

He looked toward Ready Ballard and Susie Anna, and he touched the brim of his hat.

"*Do na da go huh,*" he said. "We shall see one another again."

They had ridden only the first few miles

toward Texas. The road was wide there with a slight downward incline, and all three were sitting on the wagon seat. The two saddle horses along with the recovered packhorse were tied to the back end of the wagon.

Katharine spoke. "For my first trip away from home, it's really been quite an adventure."

"I wish it could have been less eventful," said Dhu, "for your sake, but I am glad that you're returning with us to Texas."

"Are you?" she said.

"Yes, I am," said Dhu, "and I hope you'll be staying with us for a good, long while."

"Well, I —"

Katharine could feel herself blush.

"I'd like to have plenty of time to get better acquainted with you," Dhu said.

Ben looked at Dhu with sudden realization. He opened his mouth as if to speak, but he checked himself. He could almost hear Dhu telling him that he talked too much. So he decided instead to talk to himself. Dhu Walker, he said, is getting sweet on my sister! I'd have never thought it. Never in a thousand years. And what's worse, she seems to be liking it just fine.

About the Author

Robert J. Conley, Cherokee, was born in Cushing, Oklahoma, in 1940. After finishing high school in Wichita Falls, Texas, he attended college there at Midwestern University, receiving his bachelor's degree in drama and art in 1966 and his master's in English in 1968.

Conley was an instructor of English at Northern Illinois University and at Southwest Missouri State University. He was director of Indian Studies at Eastern Montana College, Bacone College, and Morningside College, and associate professor of English at Morningside College. In addition he spent a year as assistant programs manager for the Cherokee Nation of Oklahoma.

Conley has had poems and short stories published in numerous periodicals and anthologies over the years, including some in Germany, France, Belgium, New Zealand, and Yugoslavia. His poems have been published in English, Cherokee, German, French, and Macedonian versions.

Conley's most unusual publication is perhaps the poem, "Some Lines in Commemoration of this Site: Little Maquoketa River Mounds, May 15, 1981 ." This poem was commissioned by the Iowa State Department of Transportation and published on a permanent display board at the mound site near Dubuque.

Conley's first novel was *Back to Malachi*, published by Doubleday in 1986. Since then he has had a total of fourteen novels published, several reprints including two British editions, and a collection of short stories.

His story, "Yellow Bird: An Imaginary Autobiography," received the Spur Award from Western Writers of America for the Best Short Story of 1988. The story was published in the collection *The Witch of Goingsnake and Other Stories* (University of Oklahoma Press, 1988).

Conley lives with his wife Evelyn, also Cherokee, in Tahlequah, Oklahoma, the historic capital city of the Cherokee Nation, where he is writing full time.

We hope you have enjoyed this Large Print book. Other Thorndike Press or Chivers Press Large Print books are available at your library or directly from the publishers.

For more information about current and upcoming titles, please call or write, without obligation, to:

Thorndike Press
295 Kennedy Memorial Drive
Waterville, ME 04901
Tel. (800) 223-1244

OR

Chivers Press Limited
Windsor Bridge Road
Bath BA2 3AX
England
Tel. (0225) 335336

All our Large Print titles are designed for easy reading, and all our books are made to last.